DIP'S FLAME

SATAN'S LEGACY MC
BOOK FIVE

ANDI RHODES

BLUE JOURNEY PUBLISHING

Cover Artwork - © Dez Purington at Pretty In Ink Creations

Edited by - Darcie Fisher

Also by Andi Rhodes

Broken Rebel Brotherhood

Broken Souls

Broken Innocence

Broken Boundaries

Broken Rebel Brotherhood: Complete Series Box set

Broken Rebel Brotherhood: Next Generation

Broken Hearts

Broken Wings

Broken Mind

Bastards and Badges

Stark Revenge

Slade's Fall

Jett's Guard

Soulless Kings MC

Fender

Joker

Piston

Greaser

Riker

Trainwreck

Squirrel

Gibson

Flash

Royal

Satan's Legacy MC

Snow's Angel

Toga's Demons

Magic's Torment

Duck's Salvation

Dip's Flame

Devil's Handmaidens MC

Harlow's Gamble

Peppermint's Twist

Mama's Rules

Valhalla Rising MC

Viking

Mayhem Makers

Forever Savage

Saints Purgatory MC

Unholy Soul

What the patch binds together,
let no force tear apart.
Satan's Legacy now and forever.

PROLOGUE

KENNEDY

Nineteen years old...

"Do you, Kennedy Marie Hollings, take Michael Carter Stodge to be your lawfully wedded husband?"

My hands are shaking, and I glance down at my bouquet of white and red roses to make sure the flower petals aren't giving away my nervousness. My father is staring at me from his place next to my mother in the front pew, and it should be comforting. It's anything but.

"I do," I mumble, forcing my lips to tilt into a smile.

"And do you, Michael Carter Stodge, take Kennedy Marie Hollings to be your lawfully wedded wife?"

Michael beams at me, his muddy brown irises shiny with love. Michael is a nice man, a good man, but he's... old. Not that my father sees anything wrong with that. He, with the help of the church, is the one who arranged this marriage and for him, it's more about appearances than his daughter being happy.

"I do," Michael says, his voice gravelly from years of smoking cigarettes.

The rest of the ceremony goes by fast and before I know it, I'm a married woman. I'd give anything for that not to be the case, but it is what it is.

I can't even go to the local bar and drink, but I'm a wife.

After Michael and I walk down the aisle toward the back of the opulently decorated church, he excuses himself to the restroom, leaving me to wait just outside the door. I fiddle with the new ring on my finger and watch as our many guests exit the building. The reception is being held at the country club, and there isn't a person attending who would be okay with being late.

"Congratulations, Mrs. Stodge."

"Thank you," I numbly reply to a man I don't recognize.

He's older, although only than me. Everyone present today is my parent's age or better.

Judging by the gray at the man's temples and receding hairline, I'd put him in his fifties.

So, the same age as your husband.

"I'm Henry Granger. I play golf with Michael at the club," he explains, shoving his hands in his pockets. "Every Wednesday, like clockwork, for the last twenty years."

"It's nice to meet you."

"You as well. I hope to see you at the club. Some of the wives get together while us men play," he says. "I know my wife would love it if you joined them."

Then why isn't she here asking me?

"I'd like that," I lie. "I'll have to see what my class schedule looks like first though."

That was the one and only concession that was made

for me with this marriage. Michael will pay for my college education, as long as I major in something he deems appropriate for a woman. I haven't decided what that will be yet, but I'm working on it.

I make a mental note to schedule classes so my Wednesdays are full. There is nothing appealing about spending a day with people who have more money than sense. And the thought of spending time with women who have made it their life's mission to serve their husbands fills me with dread.

What the hell am I getting myself into?

You don't have a choice in the matter, so suck it up, buttercup.

"Well, I better be going," Henry murmurs, no doubt sensing my unease.

I can be polite, but there's only so much control one can exhibit over their facial expressions. And, according to my father, that's a skill I need to work on.

"Thank you for coming to the ceremony, Mr. Granger." My words ring false, but the half-hearted expression of gratitude is the best I can manage.

He nods. "Wouldn't have missed it."

A woman with perfectly styled silver hair calls out to him from the end of the hall, and he walks away. I watch him retreat, and when he reaches her, he leans in to whisper something. They both look back at me with odd expressions, but I dismiss it.

If there's anything my life has taught me, it's that people are judgmental about things they don't understand. I'm now the nineteen-year-old wife of a fifty-two-year-old. I'm bound to get a few curious glances. It won't matter that this marriage isn't what I wanted, that I had no choice. It won't occur to others that I could possibly be unhappy.

All people will see is a gold digger, and I've accepted that.

I hold my hand out and splay my fingers. Staring at the diamond winking back at me, I sigh. People will see this rock and think I've got it made. They'll see the large home I now reside in and wonder if I fucked my way into it. They'll see my expensive wardrobe, my fancy car, and my doting husband and speculate behind my back.

They'll see me and...

Not see me *at all.*

CHAPTER 1
DIP

"We ride out in an hour!"

"Heard, Prez," I call through the motel room door.

We've been away from the clubhouse for a week now, and today is the day Satan's Legacy MC leaves its mark on Sante Fe, New Mexico. It's also the day we end a miserable human being's life, but when you fuck with one of our own, that's what you get.

None of us care that we'll be the only ones aware of what we've done. Cam Slate will be eliminated, and that's all that matters. If anyone misses the sorry sack of shit, fuck 'em. He deserves what's coming to him.

When Snow called an emergency church session last Saturday night, my brothers and I knew it wasn't to give us all a cookie for good behavior. Something bad was going down, and there wasn't a single one of us who wasn't there for it.

As I gather my belongings and shove them in my duffel, I'm startled by pounding on the door.

"Jesus," I mutter, striding to the door.

Yanking it open, I'm surprised to find Magic, the club's enforcer, standing there, a murderous glint in his eye.

"What's up?" I ask.

"What's up?" he repeats as he strides past me. "What's fucking up? I'll tell you what's up."

Rather than tell me, he begins to pace. I close the door and move to sit on the bed. Magic clearly has something to get off his chest, and I've learned to be patient at times like these. He'll spit it out eventually.

"Cam fucking Slate is *what's up*," he snarls, clenching his fists at his sides. "I just got a text from Laney."

When he doesn't elaborate, I can't help but wonder why a text from his Ol' Lady is such a big deal. And what the hell does that have to do with Slate?

Magic stops in front of me and glares. "Did you hear me?"

"I did. But I'm not real clear on what you're trying to tell me," I say honestly.

Magic growls as he pulls his cell out of his cut. He taps the screen several times and turns the device so I can read the text.

Laney: He's at it again but now he's targeting Shiloh

Tension seeps into my muscles, coiling them to an almost painful degree. Shiloh is Magic's stepson, and our Prez's nephew. Not only did Slate prey upon Prez's own stepson, but now his nephew? This guy is fucked nine ways to Hell.

"Now do you get it?" he barks.

I push up from the bed and quickly throw the remainder of my shit in my bag. After throwing it over my shoulder and tucking my gun in my waistband, I move to the door.

"Did you go to Snow with this?" I ask.

Magic nods. "Prez said to come get you so we can head out early."

"And you didn't think to lead with that?" I snap, moving to the door. "Cam's dying tonight, Magic. He can't hurt Shiloh."

"No shit, Sherlock," he seethes as he strides past me and out into the parking lot.

Shaking my head, I let the door slam shut behind me and follow Magic to the group of Harleys at the far end of the lot. The neon lights of the motel sign flicker in the dark, as does the lone streetlamp illuminating our way. The place is rundown and should probably just call it quits, but it serves a purpose, I suppose.

Its only purpose is providing a bunch of bikers a place to lay their heads at night where they won't be asked if their trip is for business or pleasure.

How do you explain to someone that we're here to take a life so it's both?

"What the fuck took so long?" Duck, our VP, demands when we reach the others.

Magic doesn't respond, and I'm not about to throw him under the bus and say he wasn't immediately forthcoming with his orders.

"Sorry," I reply as I stuff my duffel into my saddlebag. "Was takin' a shit."

Magic's eyes cut to mine, and I smirk. Yeah, fucker, I got you.

"For the love of..." Duck scowls. "No more doggie bags for you when we eat at a Mexican restaurant."

"Can I help it that the fo—"

"Now isn't the goddamn time to debate eating habits and dumps," Snow snaps. "My son and nephew are in danger, and—"

"Prez, man, they're safe," Toga, our Sergeant at Arms, says. "They're home and protected, and Slate's here in Sante Fe, none the wiser about what's coming for him."

Snow glares at Toga, then swivels his gaze to encompass us all. "Let's fucking ride."

Twenty minutes later, we're parking our Harleys on a street three blocks from Slate's house. We've spent the last week obtaining as much information about the prick as we could, and Little Man, a prospect, has been tailing him, making sure he remains close to home.

"Everyone clear on the plan?" Snow asks as we make our way through the streets.

"Get in, kill him, get out," Duck says with a shrug. "Pretty standard shit, Prez."

"Watch it," Snow snarls. "I'm not in the mood for your flippant bullshit."

I roll my eyes at their exchange. Snow and Duck are best friends, have been for as long as I've known them. But that also means they can get under each other's skin faster than anything.

"Let's just get this done," Snow says and glances over his shoulder at me. "Dip, you clear on your part in all this?"

"Crystal."

As one of the only single members left in Satan's Legacy left, it's my job to distract Slate's sister. I have to do whatever it takes to keep her from being witness to what they do to her brother. Normally, I'd flirt, even fuck the girl if necessary, but...

I shudder at the thought.

She's his much *older sister so it better not come to that.*

If I fail at my job, she dies. We're not about taking the lives of the innocent, especially when their only sin is sharing DNA with the guilty. Failure isn't an option.

And not just for my cock's sake.

When we reach the house, Snow leads the others around back, and I stroll right up to the front door to knock. It's late, but not so late that no one will answer.

The door swings open, and Elouise Slate stands there in a faded yellow nightgown, looking every bit of her sixty years. She's a sight, that's for sure.

"Hello, ma'am," I greet. "I'm sorry to bother you so late, but I'm the president of the neighborhood watch program, and I've received sev—"

"We have a neighborhood watch?"

I nod. "Oh, yes, ma'am."

Elouise leans past the door frame and looks to the left and then right before narrowing her eyes on me. "Is this a joke?"

"No, ma'am, no joke," I assure her.

"This is one of the most crime-ridden areas of the city," she says. "Since when does anyone here give a damn about the neighborhood?"

Shit.

"It's recent," I blurt. "I'm new to the neighborhood and thought it would be beneficial to start the program. We might not have much, but we need to protect what we *do* have."

She stares at me for a moment, and I expect her to call me on my bullshit, but she shocks me by nodding.

"Makes sense. So, Mr..."

"Black," I insert. "Mr. Black."

"Well, Mr. Black, why are you here?"

"As I started to say earlier, I've received several

complaints recently, and I wanted to address them with you."

"Complaints?" A thud from inside the house pulls her attention from the conversation, and she sighs before looking at me again. "Sorry about that. My brother gets loud when he plays his video games," she explains, her tone full of annoyance. "I've told him time and time again to keep it down, but does he listen? No. Ungrateful twit. I guess that's what I get for taking him in when he was released from prison."

Yeah, she's not gonna miss him at all.

"Well, ma'am, that's sort of why—"

"I was all set to retire when he was released," she continues as if I hadn't spoken. "I should be enjoying my life, traveling, but no. I'm stuck with Cam, a grown-man child with an affinity for children. But he's kin, so what was I supposed to do? I couldn't let him be homeless. Mama and Daddy taught me that family is family, no matter what they've done. So, here I am... unable to show my face in public without being called hideous names because of Cam's past. I love my brother, don't get me wrong, but I hate him too. I wish..." Elouise blinks several times and looks up at me. "I'm sorry. You don't want to hear my problems." She waves her hand dismissively. "You said something about complaints?"

Woman's got more baggage than the lost luggage department of American Airlines.

"Yes, ma'am." I smile politely. "I hate to even bring this up now, but I've received several complaints about odd noises coming from your home at all hours of the night. And some of the neighbors are also upset about the potential theft of their Wi-Fi."

Elouise squints. "The neighborhood watch cares about Wi-Fi?"

"Well, no, not Wi-Fi specifically. But we do care about theft."

We also care about men who use video games to prey on children.

And so the conversation goes. Elouise alternates between bitching about her brother being a burden and questioning my reasons for being here. I listen to her with one ear while the other is tuned into what's going on inside her home. Fortunately, she continues to attribute any noise she hears to 'Cam's childish video games'.

When, out of the corner of my eye, I see my brothers sneaking around the corner of the porch, relief washes over me. I slide my hand into my pocket and make a show of pulling out my cell phone and staring at the screen.

"... boys will be boys, I suppose, but he's thirty-six. Hardly a—"

"Ms. Slate, I really must go." I flip the phone quickly... long enough for her to think there's something important on it, but not long enough for her to actually see anything. "There's an emergency at home I need to handle."

"Oh, of course." She frowns. "I'll speak to Cam about the issues you brought to my attention. I can assure you, they won't continue to happen."

"I appreciate that. Thank you."

She nods curtly and closes the door. I rush to catch up to my brothers, meeting them at the corner.

"Are we good?" Snow asks me as we walk the few blocks to our Harleys.

"Aside from never being able to get the last fifteen minutes of my life back, yeah, we're good. Bitch hates Cam. Pretty sure she won't give a shit that he's dead."

"Great," Duck mutters. "Cause making it look like a suicide sorta went out the window."

"What do you mean?"

"Ask Prez and Magic," Toga says with a smirk.

"I don't know what you're pissed about," Magic snaps. "It's not like he's gonna need it in Hell."

I dart my eyes from Magic to Snow. "Someone wanna tell me what's going on?"

Snow reaches into his pocket and pulls out a bandana. When he unwraps it, I throw my head back and laugh because right in the middle of the fabric is a severed penis.

"Need to find somewhere to dump this," Snow says casually.

And this is why I love my life, distracting old ladies aside. Things might not always go to plan, but there's never a dull moment.

Never.

CHAPTER 2
KENNEDY

"I'm so sorry for your loss."

Unwanted guilt floods my system as I return yet another hug from someone whose false sincerity grates on my nerves like fingernails on a chalkboard. I remind myself that I have nothing to feel guilty about. My marriage was forced upon me, as was a life I never wanted.

My parents, Michael, and the church are the guilty parties.

"Thank you," I murmur, delicately dabbing at the corner of my eye to wipe a tear away.

My tears aren't for the reason most think. I should be a grieving widow, a woman heartbroken at the loss of her husband after a short battle with lung cancer. But I'm not that woman. I'm not sad in the least. My tears are born out of a happiness so great, I know no other way to express it.

I'm finally free.

"Michael was a good man," the woman says. "We'll miss him at church."

'Fuck the church' is on the tip of my tongue, but I wisely

hold it in. I've managed to survive the last ten years, and I can get through the rest of today. Once Michael is six feet under, I can let all my rage and hatred loose.

The viewing seems to last forever, but when I'm quietly escorted to my seat in the front pew, I know I'm close. I'm so damn close to an end I thought would never come.

As the pastor drones on, extolling on Michael's virtues, I let my mind wander. After the service at the church, there's a celebration of life at the country club. Once that is over, life as I've known it is too. And I'm beyond excited at the prospect.

Excited and scared as hell.

Over the years, I've managed to squirrel away money from the meager allowance Michael provided me. It seems he was willing to pay for my college degree, but when it came time to put it to use and get a job, he drew the line. I wasn't permitted to earn my own money because he was too afraid I'd use it for nefarious purposes... like leaving his ass.

He was right to be afraid. But it didn't matter.

I once had a group project in one of my college courses, and when Michael found out one of the group members was a guy, he made a call to my professor and a donation to the school, and before I knew it, I'd been excused from the assignment with an A.

Now I'm twenty-nine with a degree in nursing that came in handy with Michael's illness but that I have no desire to ever use again, a house I can't stand, and no idea what's next.

Going through the motions as I've been essentially trained to do, I make it through the rest of the day relatively unscathed. Sure, I make promises I know I won't keep, to stay in touch with people I can stand, and I lie to my parents about what my plans are now that I'm 'all alone in this sinful world', but I survive.

When I leave the country club, I point my BMW in the direction of home. It's not lost on me that all the *friends* who went on and on about being there for me, supporting me in my 'time of need' are nowhere in sight. None of them offered to follow me home to make sure I'm okay. None of them will drop off food throughout the week or call to check in because they care.

Because none of them give a damn about you.

After pulling into the four-car garage, I put the Beamer in park and simply sit. For all my musings about hating my life and my late husband, I suddenly feel... sad. I didn't expect the emotion, but I suppose it makes sense.

The life I've known is over. At least with Michael, I knew what to expect. My every move was controlled, planned for me. Even when he first got sick, he hired an assistant who became the coordinator of my days.

At first, marriage wasn't so bad. I had school as an escape, as a place to pretend I was a normal teenager going through normal milestones. But then I graduated, and there was no escape. Don't get me wrong, every second wasn't bad.

Michael never physically hurt me, he never denied me things I wanted... as long as it wasn't an inconvenience to him or something that could lead to the corruption of my soul.

Basically, I became who I am based on who he wanted me to be. I can cook, clean, organize charitable functions, and act as the perfect trophy wife, but I've never vegged out and binge-watched a show on Netflix, filled out a job application, or even gotten drunk with my best girlfriends on a bottle of wine after a boy broke my heart.

Come to think of it, I've never been drunk at all.

I don't know what my favorite color is, or food or drink or movie. I know if someone asked me those things, I'd say green, lobster, iced tea, and anything starring Glenn Close, but that's my late husband's influence.

At least you know that much.

Forcing my melancholy aside, I turn the car off and push open the driver's door. My phone rings, and before I can step out, I dig through my purse to find the cell. Without looking to see who it is, I answer.

"Hello."

"Kennedy, it's your father."

I heave a sigh. "Hi."

"I know you're grieving, but your mother and I are hosting a dinner party tomorrow, and we'd like you to be there."

Translation: your attendance is expected.

"I know you'd prefer to stay home and wallow," he continues in a judgmental tone. "But you're young, and life moves on."

"Father, I—"

"Now, your mother has invited several eligible bachelors so be sure to dress appropriately. You want to make a good first impression."

"Tomorrow isn—"

"The party starts at seven, with dinner being served at eight," he goes on. "Be at the house no later than five, that way your mother can assist you with any last-minute wardrobe changes."

Translation: your mother will be dressing you.

"I really don't think thi—"

"Better yet, I'll have our driver pick you up at your house at four-thirty. That way I know you'll be on time."

"Father, I won—"

"See you tomorrow."

When he disconnects the call, I hold the phone in front of me and glare at the screen. At least when Michael was alive, my parents backed off and let me live my life, such as it was. Apparently, that's also ended.

Rather than put my cell back into my purse, I throw it as hard as I can at the wall, and grin like a fool when it shatters. Getting to my feet, I swivel my head from side to side, searching for Michael's golf clubs. I spot them in the corner and stomp over to yank one out of the bag.

Full of indescribable fury, I lift it over my head and bring it down on the hood of the BMW. I swing that club with all my might, denting and damaging the vehicle and breaking every window before moving onto the Lincoln Michael drove before he got sick.

The only car I leave untouched is the vintage cherry-red Corvette Michael bought me as a ten-year anniversary gift. That was less than a month ago, and no one other than the two of us and Michael's assistant even knew about it. Michael was sick, and I took care of him, so there was never a reason to drive it, and I don't have any friends to show it off to.

After wearing myself out, I toss the golf club to the floor and stride to the door that leads to the house. I snag my purse as I pass it, and head straight to the master bedroom once I'm inside.

I no longer have to live the rest of my days under someone else's rule. I don't have a husband to answer to, and I'm an adult so my parents go suck on a lemon.

"Suck on a lemon," I mutter to myself. "Seriously, Kennedy?"

I stop in my tracks and tip my head back like a wolf getting ready to howl at the moon.

"Fuck, shit, damn, motherfucker, ass, bitch, ahhhhhhhh!" I shout at the top of my lungs. "My parents can go fuck themselves with a, with a... they can go fuck themselves however people fuck themselves!"

I grin, feeling calmer than I have in years.

"Huh."

Suddenly, I know what I'm going to do next.

I'm going to leave Rhode Island.

It takes me less than twenty minutes to pack up my stuff. The majority of my clothes are in a heap on the bedroom floor because I hate them, but the few pairs of jeans and t-shirts get tossed into a suitcase. I gather my toiletries and makeup and dump them in with the clothes.

Next, I move to the shoebox in the closet where I've hidden my money. I open it and count the bills, and my body deflates when I realize just how little I have.

Michael may have been rich, but I don't have access to his money. Not yet anyway. And there's no way in hell I'm sticking around to wait on the reading of the will and all that to get sorted out.

Twenty-seven hundred dollars won't last very long, not if I need to completely rebuild my life in a new location. But it'll get me out of the state, and at the moment, that's all I care about.

I put all but five hundred bucks back in the shoe box and tuck the rest in my purse. Then I add the box of cash to my suitcase. Zipping it, I wrack my brain for anything I might be forgetting and come up empty.

When I return to the garage, I toss my suitcase and

purse on the passenger seat of the Corvette before climbing into the driver's seat. I adjust the mirrors and then turn the vehicle on. She purrs to life, and I rest my hand on the dash.

"It's you and me, baby," I say to the machine. "We're gonna go find us a life and learn how to live it."

CHAPTER 3
DIP

"Hey, sugar."

Lowering my beer bottle, I narrow my eyes at Minnie. Last time I caught a glimpse of her, she was on her knees in front of one of the couches, sucking off Spark, the club treasurer. I look over her head and see Spark zipping his jeans as he heads toward the stairs, a satisfied grin on his face.

"Hey, Minnie."

As a club whore, she bounces from one cock to the next every chance she gets. Every brother knows she's trying to attach herself to one of us in order to elevate her status within the club, but it'll never happen. Those of us still unattached have zero interest in tying ourselves to second-hand pussy for the rest of our lives.

Minnie takes a step closer and presses her palm to my chest. "What're you doing standing here all alone?"

I wrap my hand around her wrist and remove her touch. I've fucked Minnie, several times but lately, club whores don't do a damn thing for me. The thought of sinking my cock into a hole that's been drilled more times than an oil reserve doesn't hold the same appeal it once did.

The more I watch my brothers find their ol' ladies, the more I wonder if there's someone out there for me. *And just me.*

"If I'm alone, there's a reason," I grumble.

Minnie bats her lashes. "C'mon, sugar," she purrs. "Why don't you take me back to yo—"

"Not interested," I snap.

"I bet I can get you interested," she says as she reaches for the button of my jeans.

"Touch me, and you'll live to regret it," I snarl.

When Minnie pouts, her bright red painted bottom lip pathetically wobbling, I roll my eyes. If I thought for a second that I'd actually hurt her feelings, I'd feel guilty. But I didn't hurt her. Pissed her off, maybe, but I can live with that.

"You're an ass," she hisses when I simply stare at her.

"Walk away, Minnie," I urge. "Before you say something that you can't take back."

She looks as if she's going to argue but then she huffs out a breath and whirls around to stomp across the room in search of a willing target. I drain the rest of my beer before turning to set it on the bar but freeze with it hovering just above the wooden surface.

Little Man, the prospect who's bartending tonight, is standing behind the counter, a grin on his face.

"What's so funny?" I demand.

His expression sobers, and he shakes his head. "Nothin', Dip."

"Clearly, it's something. Spit it out, prospect."

"Can I get you another beer?" he asks, and I shake my

head with a glare. Little Man heaves a sigh. "Minnie is entertaining, is all."

I snort. "That's what she's here for."

"But you turned her away."

"I did."

"Couldn't help but notice you turned away all the club whores tonight," he comments.

"What's it to ya?"

Little Man shrugs. "Just an observation."

"Observe less," I bark before storming out of the clubhouse.

As I walk across the compound, toward my cabin, I mull over Little Man's words. He's right about me dismissing every attempt made to flirt or get in my pants, but I'm just not feeling it... or *them*.

Maybe I'm just tired.

Yeah, tired of the same old, same old.

When I reach my place, I climb on my Harley rather than head inside. It's only ten, and the night is young. I might not be in the mood for club whores, but that doesn't mean I'm not in the mood for anything.

The ride into the city does little to clear my rapidly souring mood. I should turn around and go home, but all I'll find there is an empty cabin and deafening silence.

I ride past the shelter Satan's Legacy provides protection for, the place where Snow met his ol' lady, Sami, and spot Brady's bike parked by the curb. He's on guard duty tonight and for a moment, I debate on stopping and taking his place, but I decide against it.

Continuing down the street, I take the next right and ride around downtown for what feels like forever before parking in front of a dive bar I've never been to before. Despite never coming here before, I'm familiar with

Barlow's Bar, as I am with pretty much everything in the city. As the Road Captain, it's my job to plan routes and runs, and knowing as much as I can about streets, businesses, and potential roadblocks comes with the territory.

There aren't many vehicles on the street, but the music and chatter drifting from the open door tell me that the place is busy. It's Friday night so that's not surprising.

After stepping inside, I'm immediately hit with the haze of cigarette smoke and the smell of weed. There are two pool tables off to the left, and the bar takes up the entire wall on the right. The place is small and crowded, and just what I need.

I make my way through the small groups of customers and when I reach the bar, I lift my hand to get the bartender's attention.

"What can I get ya?" she asks after handing several bottles to another individual.

The woman is tall, taller than I prefer, but she's got a set of tits on her that I could bury my face in, and a body made for sin.

"Let's start with your number and follow that up with what time you get off," I drawl, leaning my elbows on the bar top in an effort to get closer to her.

She lifts her hand and wiggles her ring finger so I can't miss the sparkling diamond. "Pretty sure my husband wouldn't approve."

I chuckle. "Noted. And sorry about that."

I like to flirt as much as the next guy, but I don't fuck with married women. I don't give a shit how tempting they are.

"No need to apologize. I'm used to it." She smiles. "Now, what can I get ya to drink?"

"Whatever ya got on tap is fine."

She moves to the beer taps to fill a glass, returning a minute later to slide it across the bar. "Here ya go." I pull out my wallet, but before I can grab a twenty, she says, "It's on the house."

I stare at her, my forehead wrinkled with confusion. "Why?"

"Because you didn't keep trying to hit on me after you saw the ring," she says matter-of-factly.

"Why the fuck would I do that?"

"You'd be surprised at how few men give a damn about things like husbands and vows."

"Those aren't real men."

"And you're a real man..." She lowers her eyes to the patch on my cut, then lifts them again. "Dip." She smirks. "Helluva name. I'm guessing there's a story there."

"There is, but I only share that with my friends."

"Got it." Her attention is diverted to the end of the bar, and she sighs. "Be right back."

"I didn't catch your name," I call after her.

She turns around and walks backward, a grin on her face. "Jenny. Jenny Barlow," she says before swiveling to continue toward a new customer.

I watch her wait on several people, and just when she seems to be finishing with them, a woman steps up to the bar, and my lungs seize.

Holy shit!

The woman isn't wearing what I'd consider bar-hopping clothes, but she's beautiful, nonetheless. Her mint green sweater falls off one shoulder to reveal smooth, creamy skin, and her dark hair frames her face with curls. Her makeup isn't caked on, but rather it's tastefully done in a way that accentuates her full lips and perfectly sculpted cheekbones.

The woman's gaze flits from side to side like she's nervous. I watch as she orders a drink, but her hesitation is clear.

She's not your stereotypical barfly.

I can't pull my stare away from her. She's beautiful, and something tells me she doesn't even know it.

Her. I want her.

CHAPTER 4
KENNEDY

"Put her drink on my tab, Jenny."

I glance at the man sitting on the stool next to me out of the corner of my eye. He's wearing a suit, and the top few buttons of his white dress shirt are undone. I suppose he's handsome, if I wanted a man who reminds me of the country club scene. When I came into Barlow's Bar, I didn't know what to expect, but having a man offer to pay for my drink within the first three minutes certainly wasn't it.

"No thank you," I say quietly as I slide a ten-dollar bill across the bar.

The bartender—the man called her Jenny—smirks at him. "Go find someone else to hit on, Harry," she says and nods at a group of women near one of the pool tables. "Plenty of other chicks to try your luck with."

Harry glares at me before looking toward the 'chicks' Jenny directed his attention to. "Don't know what you're missing," he mutters before rising to his feet and sauntering over to the small group.

"Sorry about him," Jenny says as she takes my money. "Harry's annoying but harmless."

"It's okay."

She goes to the cash register and brings me back my change.

"Keep it," I tell her. "For sending him away."

She nods and tucks the bills into the pocket of her tight jeans. I expect her to walk away, to tend to other customers, but she doesn't. Instead, she stares at me a moment before tilting her head.

"You're not from around here, are ya?"

"What makes you say that?"

"Honey, around here, a guy offers to buy a drink for a woman, and she doesn't want him to, she tells him to fuck off, not 'no thank you'. You're... polite."

That's all I know how to be.

"You say that like it's a bad thing."

She emphatically shakes her head. "No, not at all. But if you're gonna hang out here at Barlow's, you need to *dirty* up a bit."

"Dirty up?" I repeat, glancing down at myself. It was hard enough to leave the motel in jeans and a sweater when the last ten years dictated I be dressed to the nines no matter what. "But he was in a suit!"

Jenny snorts. "I'm not talking about your clothes," she says as she grins at the sweater I splurged on earlier today after making the decision to go out. "That color is perfect for you, by the way. Brings out the color of your eyes."

She glances over her shoulder, presumably to make sure the other bartender has things handled, but she doesn't immediately face me again. I follow her gaze, and that's when I see him.

Holy smokes!

The man standing near the center of the bar has his eyes trained on Jenny, and I can't stop the jealousy that snakes through me. No man has ever looked at me that way, like he's starving and I'm the only thing that will satiate his appetite.

When Jenny turns back around, she grips the edge of the bar. Her diamond ring flashes in the dim lighting, and my jealousy deepens.

What I wouldn't give to have a husband like that.

"You're very lucky," I tell her.

Lines crease her forehead when she knits her brows. "Lucky?"

I tip my head toward the man in the leather vest. "Having a husband who stares at you like that..." I blow out a breath.

I feel like I need to take a pregnancy test just from witnessing it.

Jenny's eyes widen a split-second before she lets out a laugh. "Oh, honey, no." She lifts her hand and wiggles her finger. "This is all for show. I'm not married."

"You're not..." I shake my head. "I don't understand."

"I've owned this bar for four years now, and it took all of a month to realize that men are pigs." She smirks. "And men with liquor in their system are the slop that pigs eat."

"Wow. That's a—" I wrinkle my nose. "That's a mental image I could have done without."

"Anyway, the ring helps me judge a person's character." She glances over her shoulder. "And that man you thought was my husband... he's a good man."

"So you know him well?"

"Nope, never seen him before tonight," she says. "But he apologized for hitting on me when I showed him the ring. That doesn't happen."

"Seriously?"

I'm so out of the loop with how things work in the real world.

I might not be comfortable in a country club, but at least I know what to expect. Here... not so much.

Jenny glances over her shoulder again and then grins at me. "Why don't you go talk to him?"

"Oh, no. I couldn't."

"Why not? He was staring at you, not me."

Huh?

"Because I'm a widow," I blurt.

Jenny's face falls, and she reaches for my hand. "I'm so sorry."

"Thanks," I mumble automatically. "But it's okay. Really."

"How long were you married?"

"Ten years."

"Damn, that's rough."

I huff out a breath. "Rough. Yeah, you'd think, wouldn't you?"

She narrows her eyes. "Not a good marriage?"

"An arranged marriage."

Jenny whistles. "People still do that?"

I laugh, but there's no humor in it. "In my world... my previous world, yes."

"So, I was right," she says. "You're not from here."

I shake my head. "No. I grew up in Rhode Island, but after my husband died, I had to get out of there."

"How long have you been in town?" She waves her hand. "Ya know what? Never mind. I'm being nosey."

"It's fine, really," I assure her with a smile. "Honestly, it's nice to talk to someone who isn't judging me."

"Honey—" She presses her lips together and tilts her head. "I never got your name."

I thrust my hand across the bar, and she clasps it. "I'm Kennedy. Kennedy St—" *Nope. I never wanted Michael's last name and there's no reason to keep using it.* "Kennedy Hollings," I finish.

"I'm Jenny Barlow," she says. "And no judgment here."

"Thanks." I take a deep breath. "And to answer your question, I've been in Denver for two days. I'm hoping to stay, but I need to find a job and a place to live first."

Jenny grins. "Well, you're in luck."

"How so?"

"It just so happens I've got an efficiency apartment upstairs that's sitting empty. If you wanna stick around, I can show it to you after I close up."

"Oh, wow. That's, uh, that's very nice of you. But I should probably find a job first."

"I'm gonna go out on a limb here and say you don't have much work experience."

I bristle at her assessment. Not because she hurt my feelings, but because she's right. How the hell am I going to get a job with no experience?

"No, I don't," I admit. "I've got a nursing degree but don't really want to be a nurse."

"What do you want to be when you grow up?"

"I... well, I don't know. No one's really asked me that before." I shake my head. "Why am I telling you my life story? You've got work to do, I'm sure. I'm sorry for taking your time."

I move to slide off the stool, but Jenny's words stop me.

"We all need friends, Kennedy." I lift my eyes to hers, hating that my vision blurs from welling tears. Jenny reaches for a pen and scribbles something on a napkin before handing it to me. "Here's my number. If you decide you want to look at the apartment, gimme a call." She shrugs. "And if you don't, no worries."

"I, um... okay."

"And Kennedy?"

"Yeah?"

"Feel free to call me if you just want to talk or hang out or whatever. I'm free most days since the bar doesn't open until five."

I stare at her. "Why? Why are you being so nice?"

"Like I said, we all need friends."

With that, she turns to take care of other customers, leaving me to digest the very odd interaction we had.

Was it odd? Or do you just not know how to recognize normal?

I shove the napkin with her number on it in my purse and give one last glance to the almost full beer sitting on the bar. I'm not that crazy about beer, but when she asked me what I wanted to drink, I froze. I seriously need to figure out what I like.

And in a bar, with people staring at you, probably isn't the best place to do that.

My line of thinking has me darting my eyes toward the center of the bar, but the man I noticed earlier is gone. I'd been so tuned into my conversation with Jenny that I hadn't noticed him leave.

Guess he wasn't looking at me after all.

CHAPTER 5

DIP

"Where the fuck did you go?"

I flick my lighter and when the flame dances to life, I touch it to the end of the joint between my lips. When the paper and weed catch, I inhale deeply and hold in the smoke until my head starts to spin from lack of oxygen.

"Dip, brother, where are you?"

Blowing out a puff of smoke, I roll my eyes. "Dude, I'm in the city. Chill the fuck out."

"What the hell are you doing in Denver?" my brother demands.

I was staring at my future ol' lady until your dumb ass called.

Fuck, I don't even know the bitch's name, but that doesn't seem to matter a wit to my brain... or my heart or soul or cock.

"I just needed some air," I lie. "So I took a ride."

"And ended up in Denver?"

"Jesus, what's with the twenty questions?" I snap.

"Minnie's been looking for you."

"She doesn't quit, does she?"

"Nope," Carnie says with a chuckle. "And she won't until she's riding on the back of one of our bikes instead of our dicks."

"Look, tell her I'm not interested," I demand. "I already told her that but apparently, it bears repeating. Crazy bitch."

"I'll tell her, but I don't think it'll sink in."

After taking another hit, I sigh. "Thanks." The door to Barlow's swings open, catching my attention. "Gotta go."

I disconnect the call and stub out the joint on the brick wall I'm leaning against before sliding it into my cut pocket. The only reason I came outside was so I could take the call from Carnie, and my eyes have been glued to the door ever since. I didn't want to miss the girl in the mint green sweater.

But it's not her exiting the bar, and my shoulders slump. Three drunk chicks stumble down the sidewalk in the opposite direction, clearly having consumed more than what they can handle. Ten seconds later, the door opens again, and a man walks out with his hoodie pulled over his head, concealing himself from view. He has one hand in his pocket, and the cherry of his cigarette glows in the dark as it dangles from the other.

He stalks after them, slowly and with purpose, and the hair on my arms stands on end.

Motherfucker.

I watch the four of them carefully, my muscles coiled and my body ready to strike at the first sign of trouble. Because mark my words, there's going to be trouble.

When the man reaches the intoxicated women, who are oblivious to their surroundings, he chucks his cigarette into the street before wrapping an arm around the waist of the girl on the left. He shoves her against the wall as he simultaneously whips a blade out of his pocket and presses it against her neck.

"Let the fun begin," I mutter as I push off the wall and rush toward them, taking my gun out of my waistband as I go.

The girls are screaming, and another couple who're walking across the street whip out their cell phones and start recording the scene. I know there will be backlash if my cut is caught on camera, but I can't ignore what's happening right in front of me. Pushing thoughts of potential consequences from my mind, I force my focus on the man with the knife. Just before I reach him, he slides his hand under the shirt of his victim.

"Scream for me, bitch," he snarls, but when I shove my weapon into his ribs, he whirls around to fight, his target forgotten.

"How 'bout you scream for me," I seethe, taking my free hand and palming his face before bashing his head against the brick.

The crack of bone as it strikes the red clay reverberates through me, fueling my rage. I haul my arm back and when I strike out, connecting my fist with his nose, blood gushes over his lips. The man tries to shout, but I refuse to let his voice be heard. I deliver one punch after another, the small crowd that's gathered cheering me on.

When the pitiful excuse of a penis owner goes limp and slumps to the ground, my chest is heaving. Before I face the spectators, I tuck my gun into the front of my waistband and pull my shirt over to cover it.

"Show's over," I growl as I turn around.

People start to disperse, and I pull out my cell phone to shoot off a quick text to Snow.

Me: Need cleanup outside of Barlow's Bar... send the van

Without waiting for a response, I pocket my cell and stride to where the girl who was attacked is standing.

"You okay?" I ask.

Her friends stare at me, their makeup streaked with tears, but she doesn't lift her head to look at me.

"Darlin', I need to know you're okay."

Slowly, she peeks at me through her lashes and nods. I reach out and gently tip her head up by her chin.

"Are you sure?" Again, she nods. "Do you girls have a ride home?"

One of her friends shakes her head. "We only li-live a few blocks from he-here, so we walked." She shrugs, but her chin wobbles. "We tried to be re-responsible and di-didn't drive."

"Smart thinking."

The third girl's face hardens. "You don't have to mock us," she hisses. "We know we fucked up and if we'd driven, Tina wouldn't have been attacked and we'd be home by now and—"

"I wasn't mocking you," I say, ending her tirade. "You knew you were gonna be drinking so you left the wheels at home. That's smart."

"But if we hadn't been walking..." She glances at Tina, who's still shaking.

I slide my eyes from one girl to the next, ending with my focus on Tina. "Darlin', you did nothing wrong. You should be able to walk down the street without worrying about scum like him."

Tina holds my gaze for a second before throwing her

arms around my waist and sobbing into my shirt. Eventually, she cries herself out and steps back.

"I'm sorry," she mumbles, scrubbing at her face.

"No need to apologize." I debate having them sit on the ground while I wait for reinforcements to help me with the scumbag, but quickly decide against it. "Why don't the three of you go back inside the bar? Once I'm done out here, I'll make sure you get home safely."

"No, no," Tina says. "You've done enough."

"Darlin', I insist." I smile to soften the order. "Just go to the bar and ask for Jenny. Tell her Dip sent you."

I don't bother telling them that I don't really know Jenny, but all the bar owner will have to do is take one look at their tear-stained faces and hopefully understand why I'm sending them.

"O-okay." Tina glances at her friends. "Let's go."

I turn to watch them walk back inside, and a flash of mint green catches my attention. When the woman's eyes lock with mine, she lowers her gaze and whirls around to scurry down the sidewalk. I drop my stare to her ass, and my cock springs to life as disappointment simultaneously floods my system.

I have no idea how long she'd been standing there, no clue if she saw me beat the shit out of the guy, but the speed with which she's disappearing reminds me of one hard and cruel fact...

I'm not a good man, and a woman like her deserves more than I have to offer.

CHAPTER 6
KENNEDY

"We'll be in touch."

I flash a forced smile at the woman before making a hasty exit. This is the fourth job interview I've been on in a week, and they all end the same way: with a polite brush-off. I'm running out of cash and can only afford a few more nights at the motel before I reach the desperate phase of starting my new life. And if desperation settles in, I'll be forced to use the degree I never wanted in the first place.

You could sell your car.

And I will, if it comes to that. As I climb into the Corvette, I toss my purse onto the passenger seat. The key is already in my hand, and I fire up Ruby, loving the way her engine purrs.

I can't sell Ruby. She's all I've got.

Traffic is a nightmare, and it takes me twice as long as it should to get to the motel. By the time I park and get inside the small room, my stomach is growling, and my nerves are frayed. I glance at the clock and see it's not even one in the afternoon, and an idea strikes.

Reaching into my purse, I take out the napkin Jenny wrote her number on and my cell. Before I have a chance to second-guess myself, I dial her number and lift the phone to my ear.

"Where the fuck are you, Bryce?"

I glance at the screen and compare the number to the one on the napkin, confirming that I dialed correctly.

"Is this Jenny?" I ask.

"Who is this?" she snaps.

"Um, this..." I clear my throat. "It's Kennedy. Kennedy Hollings. We met la—"

"Shit, Kennedy, I'm sorry." There's a faint rustling and then the sound of breaking glass before she mutters, "Fuck."

"I'm sorry to bother you," I rush to say. "I shouldn't have cal—"

"No, you're fine," she says with a sigh. "I'm doing inventory, and one of my employees was supposed to be here an hour ago, but he hasn't shown. But that's my problem, not yours." She pauses to take a deep breath. "So, what's up?"

"I, um... Do you need help?"

"What?"

"Do you need help with your inventory?"

"Seriously?"

"Well, yeah," I tell her. "I mean, I was calling to see if you wanted to grab lunch or something so it's not like I'm busy. I don't mind coming to the bar and helping."

"You'd do that?" she asks incredulously.

"Sure, why not?"

"You don't even know me."

I can't stop my chuckle. "And you didn't know me when you gave me your number," I remind her. "Besides, wasn't it you who said we all need friends?"

"Touché." There's a smile in a tone, and I like knowing that I caused it. "If you're serious, then I accept. I'll even throw in a pizza for lunch if you're good with that."

My mouth waters. "Works for me."

"You're the best, Kennedy," she praises, her relief clear. "I'll see you soon."

We end the call, and I decide to change. I have no clue what inventory at a bar entails, but I doubt I need to be in dress slacks, a silk button-down blouse, and heels. After pulling on a pair of jeans, a t-shirt and hoodie, I slip into the sneakers I purchased at the outlets I stopped at on I-70.

Within minutes, I'm out the door and on my way back toward downtown Denver. Traffic has eased a bit and before I know it, I'm parking in front of Barlow's Bar. I lock the car and head to the entrance.

The door is locked, so I knock and wait for Jenny to answer. Minutes later, the door swings open, and Jenny reaches across the threshold to drag me inside.

"Thank God you're here," she says after slamming the door and locking it. "I've counted the fucking straws three times and gotten a different number each time. I'm losing my mind."

I trill out a laugh. "Point me in the right direction, and I'll dive in."

Jenny looks frazzled as she glances at the bar, and I follow her gaze. Piles and piles of straws litter the worn wood, and there are some scattered on the floor below. There are cases of beer and liquor sitting haphazardly throughout the space, post-it notes attached to the top box of each stack.

"I don't even know wh—"

A knock on the door has her throwing up her hands and

stomping to peer through the peephole. She disengages the lock and opens the door.

"Delivery for Jenny," the man on the other side says.

"That's me." She reaches into her pocket and pulls out some cash. "Keep the change," she says as she swaps the money for the pizza.

"Thanks," he says as she kicks the door shut.

When she turns around, my eyes widen. "How many people are coming to help?" I ask, nerves settling in the pit of my stomach at the thought of being around people I don't know.

"What do you mean?"

"Jenny, you're holding six boxes of pizza."

"Oh, this." She carries the food behind the bar. "I didn't know what you liked, so I ordered a bit of everything."

"I... You..." I rub the side of my nose. "That was... thoughtful."

"It was crazy," she says with a laugh. "I shoulda just called you back and asked, but that didn't occur to me until after I placed the order." Jenny shrugs. "It's all good. Left-over pizza is the best, and there'll be enough for both of us to take home. Why don't we eat and make a game plan, and then we can attack this mess?"

Slipping onto a stool, I nod as I drop my purse on the floor. "Works for me."

Jenny uses her arm to push the straws down to the end of the bar so she can spread out the pizza, and then she opens each box. The scent of marinara and cheese wafts into the air, and my stomach rumbles.

"Pick your poison. There's extra cheese, pepperoni, sausage, pineapple, meat lovers, and a supreme," she says as she points to each box.

All of them look delicious, but it's been so long since I've had pizza, I don't really remember what I like.

"Aren't you going to eat?" she asks before lifting a piece of the supreme and biting off the end.

"I, uh..." I avert my eyes and quickly grab a slice of the pineapple. "Yep."

I love pineapple so surely I'll like it on pizza.

I take a bite and immediately regret my decision. Happy to have learned something new about myself, and embarrassed that it happened in front of Jenny, I force myself to chew. But when it's time to swallow, I can't.

"Kennedy?"

"Hmm?"

"Do you want a napkin to spit that out in?" she asks, her lips twitching.

I nod, and she hands me one. There's no delicate way to spit out chewed food, so I'm grateful when Jenny busies herself getting us both a drink.

"Here." She hands me a bottle of water after twisting the cap off, and I greedily gulp half of it. "Girl, if you don't like pineapple pizza, why the hell'd you take a piece?"

Tears spring to my eyes at her innocent question, and her expression falls when the salty drops slip down my cheeks. Jenny rushes around the bar and wraps her arm around my shoulders.

"Kennedy, honey, what's wrong?"

I shake my head as I try to gather my thoughts. How am I supposed to explain to someone that I have no clue who I am? How do I make Jenny believe that I'm not crazy, just sheltered and shattered?

"Nothing... and everything."

CHAPTER 7
DIP

"What the patch binds together, let no force tear apart. Satan's Legacy now and forever."

My palms itch as I recite the club motto so church can begin. I don't want to be here, but as an officer, I'm required to be. Besides, what else am I gonna do? Go to Barlow's for the sixth straight day in a row?

Ya gotta get her outta your head.

"As you all know," Snow begins. "Dip stopped an attack on a woman outside of a bar last weekend. That fuck has been eliminated, but I'm concerned that this is a bigger problem than we first thought."

"Prez, shit like that is always gonna be a damn problem," Duck says. "Too many guys think they're fucking entitled to any pussy they want."

"And that shit won't fly in our city," Snow snaps.

"Unless we plan to stand guard on every street corner twenty-four-seven," Magic comments. "Not real sure how we're supposed to stop it."

"Which is why we're here." Prez thrusts a hand through

his hair and heaves a sigh. "We need to step up our presence downtown."

"Agreed," I add. "But there are only so many of us and an unending supply of sick fucks."

"Even if we could be everywhere all at once, business owners won't all be on board with our brand of protection," Toga says. "They'll see our cuts and run in the other direction."

"Which is bullshit," Brady grumbles. "You've got innocent people being attacked and because we wear a cut instead of a badge, they're gonna continue to be attacked."

"We might not be able to be everywhere, but cameras can be anywhere," I say thoughtfully.

"Go on," Snow prods.

"Well, a lot of businesses have security systems, but as we all know, most of them don't work for shit or are just for show," I explain. "Barlow's for example... When I asked Jenny to see the security footage from the night I took out that creep, her equipment had failed so there wasn't shit to see." I shrug. "I'm guessing that's the case for most of the smaller businesses where this kinda problem is happening."

"Okay, but how do we fix that?" Duck asks, leaning his elbows on the table.

"We offer to set up better security systems, and we monitor them at all times." I push up from my chair and start to pace. "We already have rotating shifts for the shelter's security and here at the compound. Why not add monitoring the security feeds for businesses downtown into the mix?"

"And if we see something on the monitors, how the fuck are we supposed to get to the scene in time to stop it?" Toga demands.

"I don't kn—"

"Have a rotating schedule for downtown patrol," Carnie suggests. When all eyes turn to him, he shrugs. "What?"

"If we're gonna do that, we need to discuss patching in some of the prospects," Duck says. "I don't know about the rest of you, but I don't wanna be away from home more than once or twice a month."

"Same here," Magic snaps. "With the kids..."

"I get it," Snow says with a sigh. "But I, for one, want the world to be safer for our kids." He turns to Duck. "If Daisy were old enough to go bar hopping downtown, would you feel differently? Would you be willing to be on patrol more than twice a month?"

"I'd be out there every goddamn night," Duck snarls as he presses a fist to his chest. "Fucking hell, man. I don't even wanna think about my baby girl out there with the evil that exists. Makes my heart feel all twitchy."

"Then maybe we need to figure out how to make this work and quit bitching that we can't be home every night," Snow barks.

"Are you gonna be out there, away from Sami and Lennox?" Toga asks.

"Fucking right I'll be out there." Prez slams a fist on the table. "When have I ever asked you all to do something I'm not willing to do?"

"Never."

"Exactly."

I stop pacing and return to my spot at the table, but I don't sit. "If we're gonna do this, I suggest we test it out with one business first, see how it goes."

"Lemme guess," Carnie taunts. "You wanna start with Barlow's?"

"What makes you say that?" I demand.

"Dip, you've been going to that damn bar every night," Snow says dryly. "I might not be the smartest man on the planet, but it doesn't take a fucking genius to figure out there's a reason for that." He arches a brow. "And I'd bet my patch that the reason has tits and a pussy."

"Jesus, is another one biting the dust?" Brady quips.

"I haven't bitten anything," I snap. "And so what if I am going to Barlow's because of a chick? What's it matter?"

"It doesn't," Duck says. "But if there's a woman you've got your sights set on, why haven't you told us about her?"

I throw my hands up, exasperated. "Want me to go pour us all cups of tea so we can sit here and gab like grannies? Or can we get back to business and leave my personal life outta the conversation?"

"Your personal life affects this club," Duck bites out before his expression hardens. "Trust me, I would know. In case you've forgotten, my personal life very recently blew shit all to hell around here."

"All of our personal crap has at one point or another," Snow adds. "Look, Dip, I don't give a flying fuck who you sink your dick into, but if you're stuck on some chick as bad as it seems you are, then it won't be long before you're claiming her and making her part of the family."

"Claiming her?" I huff out a laugh. "I haven't even talked to her!"

"What?" Magic asks, his lips twitching with barely concealed laughter.

Crossing my arms over my chest, I scowl. "Can we please get back to business?"

"Fine," Snow says. "But if this whole idea of yours passes the vote, we're starting with Barlow's."

"Whatever," I mutter.

"All in favor of Dip's idea, say 'aye'," Snow instructs.

The vote is unanimous. Looks like Satan's Legacy is making itself the unofficial guardians of Denver.

"Any objections to starting with Barlow's?" Snow asks, and every brother shakes his head.

"Good." Snow turns to our VP. "Duck, you and I will go with Dip to speak to Jenny. The three of us should be able to convince her this is a good idea." He turns to me. "Any issue with that?"

I swallow. Part of me wants to say yes, to shout that I shouldn't be allowed within ten feet of that bar because it only deepens my obsession with a woman I don't even know. But the other part of me, the completely fucking insane part of me, demands that I say no, that I give in to whatever mindfuck I've got going on.

"No issue, Prez."

Snow grins. "Great. We'll head out in five." He slides his gaze around the table. "The rest of you work together to come up with a schedule that'll work for monitoring more security systems, and we'll meet back here tomorrow to discuss it. Church adjourned."

Everyone files out of the meeting room, and I head straight for my Harley. Once Snow and Duck step outside, I fire up the bike and rev the engine. I don't know why nervous energy attacks my system at the thought of going to Barlow's. The bar isn't even open yet so it's not like she could be there.

"Ready?" Snow shouts over the roar of the trio of bikes.

Duck and I nod, and then the three of us take off. It doesn't take long to reach the city, and by the time we reach the bar, I've managed to calm myself down. Club business rarely stresses me out, and this is exactly that... club business.

Duck whistles after we park and cut the engines.

"That's a nice fucking car," he comments as he walks toward the Corvette parked in front of the Barlow's.

"Is this Jenny's?" Snow asks.

"I don't fucking know." I glance at the license plate and correct my statement. "I doubt it. It's sportin' Rhode Island tags."

"Well, whoever it belongs to is one lucky son of a bitch," Duck says. "If I were into cages, this is the kinda car I'd want."

"Do you need a mop for that drool?" I taunt, making my way to the entrance of Barlow's.

"Shut the fuck up," VP gripes. "You can't tell me you don't have a dream cage."

"Whatever mine is, it's not a sports car," I answer honestly. "Too small."

"Just knock on the damn door," Snow orders. "We came here for a reason, and it wasn't to talk cars."

I do as I'm told and step back between my prez and VP as we wait. A minute passes, and Duck pounds on the door. It never occurred to me that Jenny wouldn't be here. She's been here every night I've shown up. The girl's a fucking workaholic and the place opens in an hour. She's here.

"Hold your horses," a feminine voice shouts through the door.

The voice doesn't belong to Jenny, but I shrug it off. She has employees, and it makes sense that one or two would be here before opening to prep for the night ahead.

The snick of the lock disengaging is barely audible with the sounds of a bustling city around us, but all that noise disappears when the door is thrown open, and before me stands the woman with the mint green sweater.

No fucking way!

CHAPTER 8

KENNEDY

FIVE MINUTES EARLIER...

"I can't believe we pulled it off."

Smiling at Jenny, I enter the last bits of information into the bar's computer system like she showed me. It was really very easy to learn, and it feels good to be able to do work that doesn't involve taking care of someone else's personal and medical needs.

"I'm so glad I could help," I tell her after saving the spreadsheet and closing the laptop. "There, all done."

Jenny wraps her arms around me from the side and smacks a kiss on my cheek. "You are a lifesaver. I swear, as soon as Bryce returns my calls, his ass is fired." She steps back, her hand resting on my shoulder. "Hey, do you still need a job?"

Yes!

Jenny and I have talked a lot since I arrived a few hours ago, but I've been careful to leave my very unsuccessful job hunt out of the conversation. Although now that I think about it, I don't really know why. I told her about my childhood and my decade-long marriage, so she knows as much about me as anyone. But anytime I came close to talking about my employment search, I froze.

I didn't want her to think I was trying to get a handout. A job offered to me out of pity isn't what I want.

"I've been to several interviews but..."

Jenny levels her stare on me. "Kennedy, you told me that you've never had an orgasm and that you're worried about going to Hell, but when it comes to work, you clam up." She tilts her head. "Why?"

I slide off the stool and start to pace. She's right... I've opened up about so much. And she's the first person in years I'd truly consider a friend so I should stop holding back.

Before I can respond, there's a knock on the door. "I'll get that," I say quickly, rushing toward the entrance.

It doesn't even occur to me that Jenny wouldn't want me to answer the door to her business. After the last few hours, I feel like I belong here, like I'm a part of the Barlow's Bar team.

The knock turns into a pounding, and I roll my eyes. "Hold your horses!"

Behind me, Jenny snickers. "You tell 'em, girl."

When I yank open the door, my mouth drops open, and the inner hussy I didn't even know existed shivers.

Three men stare at me, but the only one I care about is in the middle, and he seems as shocked as I am that we're facing one another.

"Are you Jenny?" the man on the right asks.

"I, um... Jenny is..." I swallow and shake my head. "I'm not—"

"I'm Jenny," she says, stepping up next to me. "And this is Kennedy."

"Kennedy," the man in the middle says huskily.

"Aw, fuck," the third guy mutters as he nudges his friend with his elbow. "This is her, isn't it?"

"What?" the one who thought I was Jenny barks and darts his eyes from me to the middle man and back again. "Well, hot damn. This worked out better than I thought."

"Dip, what's going on?" Jenny asks. "You know we don't open for another hour. Figured I wouldn't see you until later."

Without taking his eyes off me, Dip says, "Uh, right. Well, this is Snow." He points to the man on the right. "And this is Duck," he says, pointing to the other guy. "We, uh..." He clears his throat. "We came to se—"

"Can we come in?" Snow asks. "I'd prefer to discuss this in private."

Jenny steps back, tugging me to the side with her, and allows them to enter. After relocking the door, she leads us all toward the bar.

"Not sure what an MC would possibly have to discuss with me, but have a seat," she says, gesturing at the stools before moving to stand behind the bar. When I go to sit on a stool, she adds, "Kennedy, you're back here with me."

"I am?" I ask, finally finding my voice.

She nods with a grin. "You are. It's not often I've got three Satan's Legacy brothers here, and as my new assistant manager, you're gonna want to be involved."

"You didn't tell me she was your assistant manager."

"Assistant manager?"

Dip and I speak simultaneously, and the other two men exchange a look that I can't decipher.

Jenny smiles. "Yes, Kennedy, my assistant manager. You've more than earned it today." She slides her eyes to Dip. "And I didn't tell you because it just happened."

"But I don't have..." I shake my head, not wanting to get

into this in front of Dip, Snow, and Duck. I force a smile at my new boss. "Thank you. I won't let you down."

A job... I have a job!

"I know."

"Great. Now that you've settled your staffing issues, can we get down to it?" Duck snaps.

Something in me snaps. Maybe it's the boost of confidence finally having a job gives me, or maybe it's the fact that when I buried Michael, I said goodbye to being walked all over. Whatever it is, I find I like it.

Whirling around, I glare at the surly biker. "Excuse me?" I place my hands on my hips. "You all came here, without any heads up, interrupted our work, and then get angry because we don't drop what we're doing and cater to your intrusion?" I shake my head. "I don't think so. Jenny has been more than accommodating and invited you in, so I suggest you show a little more patience."

"Yeah, you'll do just fine," Jenny comments with a smirk before looking at the three men. "Now that my assistant manager has put you in your place, what can we do for you?"

Snow throws his head back and roars with laughter. Feeling embarrassed, I tuck a strand of hair that escaped my ponytail behind my ear and duck my head.

"Don't do that." Dip's command is laced with heat, and I lift my head to stare at him. "Don't feel bad for putting Duck in his place. And never feel bad for speaking your mind."

"Oh, oh," Snow says, sobering. "He's right, Kennedy. Duck can be an ass, and hopefully, it'll do him some good to be reminded of that fact."

"Um, okay."

"Told ya," Jenny quips.

"Told me what?" I ask.

"That you had to dirty up a bit. Remember? If a guy does something you don't like, 'fuck off' is better than 'no thank you'." She winks and returns her attention to Snow. "I see your patch so, Mr. President, what can we do for you?"

"As you know, Dip handled a situation outside your bar last weekend," Snow begins.

A memory surfaces of Dip punching a man on the sidewalk and the man slumping to the ground. I'd stood there and watched the entire thing, torn between being appalled at his behavior and feeling an unfamiliar heat curl through me.

When Dip caught me looking, I ran like a coward.

"And I'm grateful for it," Jenny says. "I don't have too many problems here, but even when I do, the cops are no help. I'm glad he was here that night."

"Well, we'd like to make a proposition," Duck says, his attitude seemingly checked.

Jenny glances at me, and I shrug. I have no clue what that could mean. I'm new!

"We're listening," she says.

"Attacks like that aren't going to stop," Dip begins. "And they need to."

"I agree." Jenny pulls her cell out of her pocket and taps on the screen before turning it so they can look. "Not sure if you saw this or not, but there were two more attacks last night. One girl is in the hospital, and the other is dead. If there's something you can do to stop this shit, I'm on board."

"Wait a second," I say, trying to wrap my head around everything. "There were more attacks outside Barlow's?"

Maybe I don't want to work here.

Jenny shakes her head. "No. It was two blocks over, but that's still too close."

"Yes, it is," I agree.

"We'll never be able to stop all the freaks out there, but we're hoping to make a dent," Snow says. "We run this city, and it doesn't sit well that women are being hurt right under our noses."

I snort. "You run this city?"

Where the heck is this sass coming from?

"Kennedy, they're Satan's Legacy MC," Jenny explains. "If they say they run it, they run it."

"While that's true," Duck says. "We don't want you to be afraid of us. We might not work within the law, but we're not bad men. And we absolutely despise any threat to women and children."

"What does that mean?" I ask. "You don't work within the law, I mean."

"Have you ever seen Sons of Anarchy?" Jenny asks before any of them can answer. When I shake my head, she continues. "We'll rectify that soon. For now, don't ask questions you don't want answers to."

"But I do want answers," I insist.

"She's right," Dip says quietly. "But even if you did want answers, we couldn't give them to you."

I press my fingers to my temples to ease the forming headache. I know I wanted to find a new life, but this is... not necessarily what I had in mind.

What did you have in mind?

"Anyway," Snow says. "We're proposing..."

Jenny and I listen intently as Snow, Duck, and Dip lay out their plan to beef up security and make downtown Denver safer. The entire time they talk, I try to digest the information, but it's made difficult because Dip stares at me like there's no one else in the room. Even when he's talking, he talks to me and only me.

"So, whaddya think?" Snow asks when they're done.

"Do we need to decide right now?" I ask, surprised that I'm even aware that a question was asked.

Snow shakes his head. "No, but there's really no point in waiting."

"Can you give us a minute?" Jenny asks.

"Sure."

Jenny grabs my hand and drags me into the small kitchen behind the bar. She closes the door behind us and guides me to the opposite side of the room.

"Holy shit!" she exclaims.

"What?"

"I didn't get a chance to tell you, but Dip has been in here every night since *that* night."

"Okay."

"And he's been asking about you."

But why?

"I don't understand."

"Kennedy, that man has a hard-on for you, and judging by the way you drooled over him the entire time we were out there," she says, hitching her thumb toward the door. "You like him."

"I don't know him!" I remind her. "And I'm a widow."

"Weren't you the one who was just talking about how you came to Colorado to start over, to find herself, to learn how to live?"

"Well, yeah, but—"

"But nothing," she insists. "This is perfect. It's fate." Jenny bounces on her toes. "We're gonna take the club up on their offer, and as the new assistant manager, you're gonna be the contact person."

"But I don't even know what being an assistant manager means." I begin to pace. "What if I screw up? What if I can't handle it? What if—"

"Kennedy!"

I stop and whirl around to face her. "What?"

"What if it all works out?" Jenny asks softly. "What if you find exactly what you never knew you wanted?"

What if after what if plays through my mind as I consider her question. It's only been two weeks since I buried a husband I never wanted, but it's been twenty-nine years since I started living my life for everyone else but me.

For almost three decades, I followed all the rules my parents and the church set out for me. I never balked or made a move that wasn't already planned ahead of time. And where did that get me?

Lost. It got me lost in a sea of decisions that weren't my own.

The first decision I made for myself was to leave Rhode Island. The second was to stop in Colorado. And so far, so good.

Don't stop now.

"Kennedy?"

Jenny's voice pulls me from my thoughts. "Huh?"

"What's it gonna be?"

What's it gonna be? What's it gonna be?

The better question is, do I want to keep living my life in the shadow of what's expected of me, or do I want to live a life that makes me happy?

What's it gonna be?

"Let's do it."

CHAPTER 9
DIP

"That went well."

I glare at Duck, who's sitting on the stool next to me and smirking.

"Woulda gone better if you weren't such a prick," I snap.

"You're just pissed because your girl was here, and you weren't prepared for that shit," Snow drawls.

"My girl?"

"Face facts, brother," Duck says. "You're a goner." He bobs his eyebrows. "And if the way she looked at you is any indication, the feeling is mutual."

"Stuff a sock in it," I mutter.

"No tha—"

"Kennedy!"

Jenny's shout pulls my attention, and I hop off the stool. Before I can take a step, Snow grabs my arm and yanks me back.

"What do you think you're doing?"

"Jenny just shouted," I say. "What if something's wrong?"

"Fuck me," Snow grumbles. "If something were wrong, she'd yell again."

He's right. I know he's right. But the split second of fear that smacked me upside the head threw any chance of rational thought out the window.

I plop back onto the stool and rest my elbows on top of the bar. "I wish they'd hurry up."

"What the hell is wrong with you?" Duck asks, slapping me on the back. "I've never seen you so twisted up over a chick before."

I'm saved from answering when the door to the kitchen opens and Jenny and Kennedy walk out. Both their gazes land on me, but the giant grin on Jenny's face is a far cry from the look of unease on Kennedy's.

"We've talked it over," Jenny begins when they're standing across from us. "And we're in."

"Really?" I ask, relief sinking into my bones.

I'll never admit out loud that I was worried they'd say no and I'd never see Kennedy again, but fuck, I was sweatin' bullets.

"Really," Kennedy says. "But I do have some concerns."

Dammit.

"Maybe we can ease your mind," Duck says with a smirk. He glances at me and winks, and I know he's going overboard so I have no reason to call him a prick again.

"My first concern is the expense of all this." Kennedy waves her hand absently. "Jenny runs a very successful bar, but additional costs are going to have to come from somewhere, and we can't make a determination as to where if we don't have an amount."

I dart my eyes from Kennedy to Jenny and see the look of respect on the bar owner's face. When we first got here, it seemed as if there were some underlying issues at play when she offered Kennedy the job, but it's clear now that she's glad she did.

"That's the thing," Snow begins. "There is no expense to you. The club will cover the cost of the security upgrades, as well as the manpower to monitor the system and handle any *problems* that arise."

Suspicion flashes in Kennedy's eyes, and she crosses her arms over her chest. "Why would you do that?"

"Because this is our city," I say simply. "We have kids and families to protect. Part of that is making sure the world is a safe place for them to live in."

"You have kids?" she asks, disappointment in her tone.

I grin. "No. No kids." Her eyes drop to my hands which are resting on the bar. "And no wife, if it's a ring you're looking for."

"And he's back," Duck quips.

Jenny stifles a laugh by covering her mouth with her hand, and Snow coughs to cover up his. I, on the other hand, elbow Duck as hard as I can without taking my eyes off Kennedy. Her expression is a confusing mixture of sadness and curiosity.

"How do I know you're telling the truth?" she asks. "Jenny wears a ring, but she's not married so what's to stop you from being married and *not* wearing one?"

My mind flashes back to my first conversation with Jenny, the one where she used her 'wedding' ring as a deterrent. She's since told me she's not married, not that it matters. As soon as I laid eyes on Kennedy, it wouldn't have mattered if Jenny was hitched or not.

"Clearly you know nothing about bikers," Snow says. "Don't get me wrong, not all men who wear cuts give a damn about shit like loyalty, faithfulness, and vows, but we do. Satan's Legacy brothers won't step out on their ol' ladies. Once a woman is claimed, that's it."

"That is so fucking hot," Jenny gushes.

Duck and Snow both chuckle.

"Kennedy, I'm not married. I'm not attached to anyone," I tell her. "And if I were, I wouldn't be sitting here with a hard-on for a chick I don't even know."

"Told ya," Jenny says.

Kennedy's eyes are wide with shock, and she rubs her forehead. "This is all so confusing."

"Look, it doesn't have to be," Snow states. "We came here on business so let's stick to business. Are there any other concerns you have?"

Jenny and Kennedy exchange a look before Jenny responds. "No. The financial aspect of it was the only lingering question."

"Good." Snow pushes up from the stool and stands. "I'll send someone by tomorrow to start the installation. If that works for you, that is," he tacks on.

"Actually, I have an appointment I can't get out of," Jenny says.

"I can be here," Kennedy adds, then glances at Jenny. "I mean, if you're okay with me handling it."

"Absolutely," her boss says.

"That's settled then." Snow grins. "I saw on the door that you open at five, so I'll make sure my guys are here around ten if that works. That way, if there are any problems, there's time to handle it before you open."

"I'll be here," Kennedy confirms.

"Perfect." Duck rises to his feet. "We'll get outta your hair then."

I hesitate, wanting to ask Kennedy out but not wanting to scare her. Not wanting to send her running for the hills wins out, and I get to my feet and follow my brothers outside.

"You're seriously just gonna walk away?" Duck asks as he straddles his Harley.

"Leave it alone, Duck," Snow snaps. "Now that they've agreed to work with us, Dip will have plenty of opportunities to talk to Kennedy again. If he wants to pussy out now, that's on him."

"I'm not being a pussy," I protest. "I'm biding my time."

"If telling yourself that makes you feel better..."

Duck fires up his bike, letting his words hang in the air like a dare. A triple dog dare, in fact. But I don't take the bait, instead choosing to straddle my own bike.

Maybe a ride will clear my head.

And maybe pigs will start to fly.

While I'm stuck in my head, Snow and Duck pull away from the curb. I watch them ride down the street as I start my Harley. But before I can even get the kickstand up, the door to Barlow's flies open, and Kennedy steps out onto the sidewalk.

We stare at each other for a moment, as if looking away will break whatever invisible thread tethers us together.

Kennedy breaks first and drops her chin.

"Don't," I order, my tone gruff. "Don't hide yourself from me."

Slowly, she raises her head and looks me in the eye. She twists her hands nervously but doesn't avert her gaze again.

"You came out here for a reason, Kennedy," I say. "What was it?"

"I, um..." She swallows, and my eyes are drawn to her slender throat. "I have a question."

"Shoot."

"Jenny thinks... I mean, Jenny said..." Kennedy shakes her head as if to unjumble her thoughts. There's a war going on behind her caramel irises, and I'm dying to know what's causing it. "I'm trying to..." She groans. "This is a lot harder than I thought."

"That's okay. Take your time."

"Right. My time," she mutters bitterly, but then she squares her shoulders and hardens her expression. "That *is* right. It's *my* time."

Doubt starts to creep in because she's not making any sense. Maybe my soul cried out for the wrong woman. Maybe *I* should be the one running for the hills.

"I want you to teach me how to live," she blurts.

And maybe my soul got it exactly fucking right.

CHAPTER 10
KENNEDY

"I'm gonna need you to repeat that."

What was I thinking, blurting that out like that?

I rapidly shake my head and start backing up. "Forget I said that."

Dip is off his motorcycle so fast, I don't even have time to blink. I continue to retreat, and he advances, backing me against the wall.

"What did you mean, you want me to teach you how to live?" he asks softly, almost as if he's afraid he'll scare me if he talks too loudly.

"Please forget I said that," I plead. "It was stupid."

"It's not stupid."

"It is!" I cry. "I'm twenty-nine years old and asking a stranger to teach me about life. That's pretty stupid."

Dip leans forward, bracing his arms on either side of my head. I breathe in the scent of leather and oil, and my head spins from the intoxicating combination. I'm so far out of my league with this man, but that doesn't stop me from wanting to learn from him.

I left Rhode Island wanting a new life, and this is it.

What if you find exactly what you never knew you wanted?

Jenny's words return to my mind, a stark reminder that I had a plan when I raced out of Barlow's. I had one thought on my mind, one goal, and that was to get this man to agree to teach me his ways.

His very sinful ways.

"I'm waiting," he prods.

I sigh. "Jenny said you came back here, looking for me."

"I did."

"Why?"

Dip straightens, dropping his arms to his side. "Because I saw you the other night and something..."

"Something what?"

Like the curtain at intermission at the opera, a wall slides into place over his expression. "You explain what you meant, and then I'll answer that question," he says.

"I don't know how to explain it," I hedge.

"Try."

I'm not sure how I feel about another man bossing me around, but it doesn't grate on me quite like it did when Michael issued demands, so I let it pass.

"I'm a widow," I begin, and his eyes widen. "Married at nineteen and widowed ten years later." He opens his mouth to speak, but I hold up a hand to silence him, knowing that if I don't spit this out, I never will. And also not wanting to get into the nitty-gritty details of my marriage just yet. "I've never really..." I swallow and try to gather my thoughts. "I was young, ya know? There are so many things that I've never experienced, and I want to. I *really* want to."

"Things like what?" he asks.

Like great sex and getting drunk and riding a motorcycle and...

So many things.

"I don't know," I lie.

"Bullshit."

"What?"

"Bullshit," he repeats. "You know what you want to experience, so tell me."

"I..."

I lower my chin, but Dip lifts it gently with his finger, forcing me to look him in the eyes. "I've already told you not to hide from me."

"I know."

"Then why do you keep doing it?"

"Because this is humiliating."

"Did I do anything to make you think I was laughing at you?" he asks.

"No."

"Have I made fun of anything you've said?"

"No."

"Then it's only humiliating in your head," he says. "Sometimes you just have to say what's on your mind, consequences be damned."

"That's just it," I counter. "I don't know anything other than the consequence of my soul being damned to Hell."

Dip stiffens, and his jaw tics. "Who the fuck said you were going to Hell?"

"Everyone." I take a few deep breaths. "For as long as I can remember, if I didn't do things just right, or I went against my parents or the church or Michael, I was told that eternal damnation was my fate."

"Michael the husband?" I nod. "Bastard's lucky he's already dead," he bites out.

I sputter a laugh. "What?"

"Look, I've done some shitty stuff in my life." He points to the patch on his leather vest. "I'm in a one-percenter MC so that shouldn't be all that surprising. And I'm okay with the shit I've done. But you..." Dip shakes his head. "I don't buy for a fucking second that you could ever do anything that would send you to Hell. And anyone who made you think otherwise is a piece of garbage."

"But you don't even know me."

"All a man has to do is look at you and know you're pure good, through and through."

And that's the problem.

I chew on the inside of my cheek, and Dip grins. "Spit out whatever's in that pretty head of yours."

"What if..." I sigh. "What if I don't want to be good? What if I want to just be me, whatever that looks like?"

"Then be you," he says.

"It's not that simple."

"Why not?"

"Because I don't even know who I am. I've spent my entire life living for other people, doing what's expected of me. Shit, I didn't even know what kind of pizza I liked until today."

Dip's grin spreads. "You just swore."

I think back to what I said and realize he's right. "So?" I say stubbornly.

"It felt good, didn't it?"

"Maybe."

"Foul words sound good coming from this mouth." Dip runs his thumb over my bottom lip, and my stomach clenches at his touch. "I think I wanna hear a whole lot more come outta this mouth."

"You... you do?"

He nods. "Tell me how I can teach you how to live, Kennedy."

Dip's voice is deep, commanding, and makes my toes curl.

Take a deep breath, I spit out the first thing that comes to mind. "I wanna learn how to have sex."

"You were married for a decade, and you're a virgin?" Despite the awkwardness of the question, there's surprisingly no judgment in his tone.

"I'm not a virgin," I tell him. "But I've only ever been with Michael, and that was... not fun."

"I take it Michael was boring as fuck."

I can't stop the snort that escapes, and Dip smiles. "He was in his fifties when we got mar—"

"Holy shit, his fifties?"

"Yep."

"There's gotta be a story there."

"Not one I want to get into right now."

"Okay, but... Are you sure he's dead? You're not running from an abusive husband, are you? There's not gonna be trouble barking at your heels?"

This is the first hint of hesitation I've seen from him, and it makes me question my sanity.

"Yes, he's dead. No trouble following me, unless my parents decide it's worth their time and energy to track me down," I snap. "But then they'd have to admit to the church that their perfect daughter is no longer falling in line like she's supposed to, so I don't see that happening."

"There is so much to unpack in that statement," he says and presses his finger against my lips when I open my mouth. "But it can wait."

"Thank you."

"And I'm sorry if I upset you."

"It's fine."

"It's not, but my club is my life. They're my family, and

I'd need to warn them if there was a shitstorm coming their way."

"No shitstorm."

Dip grins again. "Really fucking good hearing you swear."

I smirk. "I'm trying. It's hard to break a lifelong habit of goodness and obedience."

"And that's where I come in."

Wait... what?"

"Huh?"

"I'll help you, Kennedy." Dip cups my cheek. "I'll teach you my sinful ways... in the bedroom and out of it. But I have conditions."

There's always conditions.

"What are they?" I ask, narrowing my eyes at him.

"First, if we do this, there will be no other men."

"Okay. But then no other women."

"Done."

"What's your second condition?"

"That one's a bit trickier."

"Okay."

"I'm gonna need you to trust me."

"I'm having this conversation with you. I feel like that shows the level of trust I have."

"Or you're just putting on a brave face because you think slumming it with a bad boy will somehow ease the pain of whatever shit you've been through."

Wow.

"Dip, I've been told my entire life how to act, what to eat, what to say, and how to dress. I've been taught that anyone who doesn't go to church three times a week or subscribe to the same beliefs shoved down my throat for as long as I can remember is bad," I explain. "You're right that you'd be considered bad. But I ran from the life that taught me that, and I have no interest in returning. I might have been forced to think one way, but that doesn't mean that I believe it was the right way. I'm not judging you by the clothes you wear or the lifestyle you live, so please don't judge mine up until this point."

"Good answer."

"It's the truth. Lying is one thing I have no interest in learning how to do. You'll always get the truth with me."

"Always?"

"Yes."

"Why me?" He arches a brow. "And remember, you just said you'd always be honest."

"Because you are the exact opposite of my old life. Because Jenny seems to think you're a good man, and she's the only friend I've got, so I'm trusting her. And because..."

"Because?" he prods.

"Because I'm very attracted to you, and even though that scares me, I want to be scared. I want to test my limits. I want to push the boundaries of polite society. I want to fucking live."

Dip growls. "God, that's hot."

"I'm glad you think so," I quip. "I need this, Dip. And here's another kernel of honesty for you. If you say no, I'll find someone else who will say yes."

"The fuck you will," he snarls.

"Yeah, I will. Because I need this. For me to be whole, for me to be *me*... I *need* this."

The longer I stand here with him, the more confident I feel. The more we interact, the less I question my sanity. The need to figure out this thing called life becomes all that matters.

And for some strange reason, the soul I've tried so hard

to keep pure is screaming at me that only Dip can help me do that.

Only Dip can dirty me up without damning me to Hell.

“We’re doing this,” he says, heat in his tone. “And I promise you, by the time you feel whole, the thought of ending our *arrangement* will leave you feeling very empty.”

CHAPTER 11
DIP

"What took you so long?"

I push past Snow and Duck, making my way to the bar at the clubhouse. After the conversation I just had, I need a fucking drink.

"Dip, Prez asked you a damn question," Duck barks, both of them hot on my heels.

"I need a goddamn minute," I snap, heading straight behind the bar to get my own shot.

Little Man watches me intently as I pour myself a double shot of Jack Daniels and slam it back. He looks like he wants to say something, but he wisely keeps his mouth shut.

"What the fuck happened after we left?" Snow demands, no longer showing any restraint when it comes to getting answers.

"Hold up," Duck inserts. "Are we gonna need a drink for this?"

"Probably," I mutter. "Although there's not enough alcohol in the world that can make it make sense."

While I was talking to Kennedy in front of Barlow's, her

proposition lit a fire inside of me, but now that I've got some distance, I can't help but wonder what the fuck I'm doing.

"Jesus, this can't be good," Duck gripes and looks at Little Man. "Pour us all something strong, prospect."

Little Man goes about following orders and after he sets three drinks on the bar, he makes himself scarce.

"Spill," Snow demands.

"Kennedy came outside after you two left," I say.

"Okay. Did you ask her out?" Duck asks.

"Not exactly."

"What'd she want? Is there a problem with the new partnership already?"

"No, nothing like that."

In unison, the three of us lift our glasses and gulp down the liquor.

"Then what the hell is it, brother?" Duck barks. "You're draggin' this out, and I gotta say, it's annoying as fuck."

Why is this so hard?

"She propositioned me," I spit out.

"Propositioned you?" Snow asks slowly. "Like for sex?"

"Among other things."

"Holy shit!" Duck grins. "What the hell is the problem then? You like the girl, she wants to bang you... seems like a win-win to me."

Snow slaps Duck on the back. "Slow your roll, VP. He said, 'among other things'." Prez slides his gaze to me. "What are the *other things*?"

I take a deep breath and try to formulate the words. "She asked me to teach her how to live."

Duck rears back, his eyes comically wide. "What the shit does that mean? Bitch don't know how to breathe?"

Hearing him call Kennedy a bitch snaps something

inside of me. I lunge across the bar at my VP, knocking our empty glasses to the floor, and we collapse in a heap of testosterone.

"Call her that again, and I'll knock your goddamn teeth down your throat," I snarl, my hand around Duck's throat.

"Dip!" Snow shouts. "That's enough!"

My chest heaves with fury as I shove off of Duck and rise to my feet. He remains on his back for a moment, staring at me in disbelief, and guilt envelopes me. I'm normally not a hothead, and he didn't do or say anything any one of us hasn't done or said, but apparently, Kennedy is my kryptonite.

I extend a hand to help him up, and Duck takes it. After I haul him to his feet, I slap him on the back.

"Sorry, VP."

Duck narrows his eyes at me and scowls. "I'll let it slide this time, but do that again, and the next vote we'll have in church is whether or not to strip your patch," he seethes. "Understood?"

"Understood."

"Now that the pissing match is over," Snow begins. "I'd really like to hear more about this proposition Kennedy made."

Rolling my eyes, I face my prez. "I don't even know how to explain it. She asked me to help her live, like I said."

"I'm still not clear on what that means," Duck adds, and I shoot him a glare. He holds his hands up and smirks. "I'm not trying to start shit, I swear. But how the hell did she get to be her age and not know how to live." He shakes his head. "It makes no sense."

"Apparently, she's been very sheltered. Raised in a church to believe that anything she does that doesn't conform to what they expect of her is sending her straight to Hell."

Snow's expression hardens. "Who's 'they'?"

I shrug. "Her parents, her husband, the ch—"

"She's married?" Duck demands.

I shake my head. "Widowed."

"Damn," Snow mutters. "That's rough."

My brows knit. "Maybe. I kinda got the feeling that she isn't too broken up about it."

"So she was married and sheltered," Duck recounts. "Now she's a widow and what? She wants to hang with a biker to see how the other half lives?"

"She wants to experience things she's never experienced," I explain, knowing it sounds weird.

Kennedy explained it so well, but I don't have a knack for words, and I don't want to betray her trust by revealing too much.

Too late.

If you can't trust your brothers, then you can't trust anyone.

"Basically, I'm going to help her have those experiences," I continue. "I already agreed."

"Can we get back to the sex part of this?" Duck asks, a grin on his face. "Because that's the part that sounds really interesting."

"Is that all you ever think about?" I ask, not at all surprised that he's coming back to that.

Duck shrugs. "It's pretty high on the list."

"I thought when you were married, that shit was supposed to taper off."

"Dip, my man, you've got a lot to learn," Snow says with a chuckle. "Fucking is great but fucking your ol' lady... that's perfection."

"Well, Kennedy isn't interested in a relationship," I tell

them. "So I don't think I'll be finding that out for myself any time soon."

"Wait," Duck says. "You get to have no-strings-attached sex with a woman you're clearly into, and you sound upset about it. What the fuck is wrong with you? That's every man's fantasy."

"What's every man's fantasy?"

"Yeah, I'd like to hear this too."

Duck and Snow whirl around at the sound of their ol' ladies' questions, and I can't stop the roar of laughter at the way their shoulders slump like kids who got caught with their hands in the cookie jar.

"I can't wait to hear this," I mutter.

"Snow, honey," Sami says with a saccharine-sweet smile. "What's every man's fantasy?"

"You are," Snow says.

Sami arches a brow. "I wasn't born yesterday."

"Of course not. But, uh... it's club business."

Grace, Duck's ol' lady, glares at my VP. "Please explain how fantasies are club business."

Duck cracks like an egg, unable to lie. "They're not," he says with a sigh. "We were talking about this woman Dip likes and how she asked him to teach her about life and sex, and I was just being a dick." He reaches out to touch his wife, but she backs away. "You are my only fantasy."

Grace and Sami exchange a look before they both bust up laughing. When she sobers, Grace smiles at Duck. "Nice save."

Sami steps between the two men and slips onto a stool. "So, Dip, tell us about this girl."

"Nope." I shake my head. "Not doing it. I can't have this conversation with chicks."

I walk away, their laughter trailing after me until I exit

the clubhouse and the door bangs shut. As I'm crossing the property to my cabin, I pull out my cell phone, wishing I would've gotten Kennedy's number.

We never made plans before she escaped back into Barlow's after we talked, and despite my reservations, I want to get started. I know I might live to regret it because if either of us is going to wind up hurt at the end of this, it's going to be me, but that doesn't seem to matter. Not really.

She'll be worth the pain.

I have no idea how I know that, but I do. I know it as sure as I know my given name is Carson Willis.

Fortunately, Jenny and I exchanged numbers when I returned to the bar to escort the three drunk girls home last weekend, so I fire off a quick text.

Me: Hey Jenny. It's Dip. What's Kennedy's cell number?

Barlow's is open for business, so I'm surprised when my phone pings almost instantly with her reply.

Jenny: Why?

Me: Wanna talk to her about the security setup tomorrow

Jenny: Is that all you want to talk to her about???

Me: Yep

Jenny: R U sure about that? You don't want to talk to her about your little chat earlier?

Well, shit.

Jenny: Yeah... she told me.

Me: Okay. So can I have her number or not?

Jenny: Under one condition...

Me: What is it with women and conditions?

Jenny: From what K said, you had some conditions of your own

Me: Fine. What's the damn condition?

Jenny: Don't break her heart. I know I haven't known her long, but she's been through a lot and deserves the best

Me: I won't break her heart

Jenny: Promise?

A growl rumbles from my chest as frustration settles in. There's nothing I can say that will convince her that Kennedy is safe with me. Or her heart is, at least. So I don't even bother to try.

Me: Are you gonna give me the number or not?

Jenny: If U hurt her, I'll kill you... 401-555-4145

Me: I owe you one

Jenny: Yeah, you do... oh, and she's off at midnight

I enter Kennedy's number into my contacts and hit save. I'd planned on calling her now, but I think I'd rather wait and surprise her later. It's harder to back out of a deal in person.

Yeah. That's much better.

CHAPTER 12
KENNEDY

"Would you hurry up?"

I force a smile at the customer glaring at me from across the bar. Jenny asked if I wanted to dive right into work tonight, and clearly, I was mistaken to agree. I'm not cut out for this.

"If you've got a problem with the service, feel free to take your business elsewhere," Jenny says after she steps up next to me.

The man shoves the twenty he's holding into his pocket and storms away and out of the bar. My face falls, and tears spring to my eyes.

"I'm so sorry," I say, facing Jenny. "Maybe I'm not cut out for this."

Jenny rests her hands on my shoulders. "Honey, it's fine. It's one customer. And it's your first night. Don't sweat it."

It isn't just one customer. That was the fourth customer to leave unhappy. And all because of me. Jenny is either the most understanding person in the world, or the worst businesswoman on the planet.

"I think I should stick to everything else and leave the bartending up to, well, the bartenders."

"And I think you should cut yourself some slack." Jenny smiles. "It takes time to figure out a rhythm. You'll get there." She swipes at the tear that spilled over my lashes. "Now, go take a quick break, recharge, and when you come back, things will look better." She reaches into her pocket and pulls out a key before handing it to me. "Here. This is for the apartment. Why don't you go check it out?"

"But you were gonna show me after work."

She winks and squeezes my shoulder. "No worries. Go have a look, and we can talk about rent and shit later."

I nod, grateful for this woman, this angel. I've never met anyone like her, and I'm pretty sure I never will again.

With the key in my hand, I walk through the kitchen and up the stairs to the apartment. Jenny explained earlier that there are two entrances. One inside and one from the back parking lot. After the attacks on women in the city, I doubt I'll ever use the one in the back.

Slipping the key into the lock, I turn it, and my heart stutters at the click of the lock disengaging.

This could be home. My *home.*

After pushing open the door, I step inside. Jenny wasn't lying. The apartment is an efficiency. There's a small kitchenette with a dorm-sized fridge, one burner stove, and tiny sink. The round table has three mismatched chairs, and the living area sports an old loveseat with a worn coffee table.

I cross the room to peer on the other side of a partition and find the bed. It's a double, which is perfectly fine. I'm only one person, so no need for anything big.

Unless Dip stays over to teach you things.

I shiver at the thought. I still can't believe I asked him,

well, what I asked him. It made sense at the time, but now? Not so much.

I promise you, by the time you feel whole, the thought of ending our arrangement will leave you feeling very empty.

Dip's words have plagued me since the second they left his mouth. What did he mean? Does he want more than what I'm willing to offer?

No. He can't. There's no way. We don't even know each other.

That didn't stop you from propositioning him.

Groaning at my indecision, I move away from the bed and check out the small bathroom. There's a standup shower, toilet, and sink. The vanity is practically non-existent, but there is a medicine cabinet, and I don't have much, so it'll work.

The apartment isn't much bigger than the motel room I've been staying in, but it's cleaner and a heck of a lot closer to work.

Work.

I still can't believe I have a job. At least for now... if I don't screw it up.

I turn on the sink and splash water over my face. My negative attitude has got to go. I left Rhode Island because I wanted a new life, and that's exactly what I'm getting. In less than twelve hours, everything is starting to slide into place. Sure the pieces are a little jagged, a little wobbly, but that'll change.

I just have to give it time.

After a quick glance in the mirror to make sure I look halfway decent, I exit the apartment and return to the bar for the rest of my shift. While I'm dealing with customers, my mind reels.

If the price is right, I'd love to live above Barlow's, but I have to talk to Jenny first. She might have a number in mind that simply isn't doable, and then I'll have to figure something else out.

The hours tick by, and I don't piss off any more people. I might be a bit slower than Jenny, but I take a page out of her book and talk while I serve, which seems to help a lot. By the time eleven thirty rolls around, my feet are killing me, my head is spinning from all the knowledge I'm soaking up, and my back aches.

But I'm happy. For the first time in a long time, I'm smiling, and it's not forced or fake. It's real. The lightness in my chest and the hope in my heart are real.

Jenny elbows me, pulling me from my thoughts.

"Well, well, well, look what the cat dragged in."

I follow Jenny's gaze and see Dip striding across the room. His eyes are laser-focused on me, and my breath catches.

"What's he doing here?" I ask.

"I told him you were done at midnight."

I whip my head to gawk at her. "But we don't close until two."

Jenny shrugs. "And the crowd has died down. Besides, you've had a long day."

"You've had a longe—"

"Hello, ladies," Dip greets when he reaches us.

"Hey, Dip. Fancy seeing you here," Jenny quips.

"I'm sure," he drawls with a smirk before returning his stare to me. "Hi, Kennedy."

"Hi."

"Can I get a beer?"

"You came here for a beer?" I ask stupidly.

"I came here for you," he clarifies. "But you've got

twenty minutes left before your shift ends, so I'll have a beer while I wait."

"Oh, um, okay."

"I'll leave you to it, K," Jenny says as she walks to the other end of the bar to deal with the few customers remaining.

In my haste to put some distance between us, I don't even ask him what kind of beer he wants.

Idiot.

I grab a bottle of Coors from the cooler and wipe off the condensation before returning to stand across from him.

"I hope this is okay," I say as I hand him the bottle.

"Is it cold?"

"Yes."

"Then it's perfect."

Dip tips the beer to his lips, and my eyes zero in on the way his throat bobs when he swallows. When he's done, he sets the bottle down and levels his gaze on me.

"So, whaddya wanna do tonight?" he asks.

Heat swirls in my belly at his suggestive tone. The sensation is unfamiliar, but not unwelcome.

"I was thinking we could just hang out," he says when I don't respond. "Keep it simple for now."

"H-hang out?"

"Yeah. Hang out. Ya know, two people spending time together doing... whatever."

"I know what hang out means."

"Then what's the problem?"

"I'm just... You confuse me."

"How so?"

"Earlier, when we talked, you seemed interested in a lot more than hanging out."

"So did you."

"I was." I shake my head. "I mean, I am, but..."

I avert my stare, and Dip reaches across the wood to grab my hand. Electricity zings up my arm, making me want to pull away and hold him forever all at the same time.

"Kennedy?"

"What?"

"If you can't tell me what's on your mind, this will never work."

I huff out a breath. "It's not that easy."

"Sure it is." Dip uses his free hand to grip my chin gently, forcing me to look at him. "I wanna bury myself in you so deep that you don't know where I stop and you begin. I wanna learn every single detail about your life, your dreams, your desires, and help you discover all the new things you want to discover. I want you, all of you." He grins and shrugs. "See, easy."

How does he do that? How does he make me want to latch on to his filthy words and promises? How does he know exactly how to make my mind spiral out of control and feel insanely calm within the span of a few seconds?

I take a deep breath. "I'm interested in more than hanging out. But this is all new to me, and I need you to be patient. I'm not used to speaking my mind let alone having someone around who gives a damn about what I have to say."

"I can be patient."

"Good."

"So, wanna hang out tonight?"

"You're relentless," I accuse, but there's no heat in my tone.

Dip tilts his head, his expression thoughtful.

"Do you want me to back off?" he asks.

Honesty... he wants honesty.

"No."

He releases my hand and flattens his palms on the bar with a giant grin.

"Then buckle up, buttercup, because shit's about to get real."

CHAPTER 13

DIP

"I can't believe you're still here."

I set the cue stick on the pool table, abandoning the four balls I had left to sink. When midnight rolled around, there'd been a slight spike in business, so Kennedy stayed to help Jenny. I didn't want to hover, so I've been shooting some pool by myself to kill time.

"Why wouldn't I be here?" I ask, arching a brow at Kennedy, who's standing a few feet from me.

"Because it's late."

I pull my cell out of my pocket and glance at the screen. "It's one thirty in the morning." I shrug. "That's early."

"Well, I'm gonna have to take a rain check on hanging out," she says. She tries to stifle a yawn but fails miserably. "I'm exhausted."

"I can see that." Tucking a strand of hair behind her ear, I smile. "Why don't you let me take you home? You shouldn't be driving when you're this tired."

Kennedy averts her gaze. Dammit, I wish she'd quit doing that. Unlike every other time, I don't call her out on it though. She wants patience, and that's exactly what I'm going to give her.

Even if it kills me.

"I appreciate the offer, really, but I'll be fine." She's still not looking at me, and there's something in her tone, something... off.

"Maybe so, but I'm not willing to risk it." I close the distance between us and wrap an arm around her shoulder. "C'mon, Kennedy. You're practically dead on your feet. Let me take you home."

"I... I don't have a home," she says, so quietly I almost don't hear her.

"Where have you been staying?"

"A motel just outside of the city. I'm pretty sure I'll be moving into the apartment above the bar, but Jenny and I haven't had a chance to talk about rent or anything yet, and my clothes are all at the motel anyway, so..."

"Yo, Jenny!" I call over my shoulder, taking matters into my own hands.

Jenny finishes with the last customer left before coming to join us by the pool table.

"What's up?" she asks.

"The apartment upstairs," I begin. "What's the rent?"

"Dip," Kennedy hisses. "I can handle this."

"Never thought otherwise," I say absently. "So, Jenny... the rent?"

And because she clearly cares more about Kennedy than me, Jenny grabs Kennedy's hand and tugs her away from me. They cross the bar and sit on two stools to have a conversation that should've already happened.

Ten minutes later, Kennedy throws her arms around Jenny and hugs her tight. When she releases her, she makes her way back toward me, her beautiful smile firmly in place.

"All settled?" I ask.

"Yeah. And... Thank you."

"For what?"

"For making us figure that out."

"I didn't make you do anything." I shrug. "I just nudged you in the right direction."

Kennedy sighs. "Well, whatever. I appreciate it nonetheless."

"So, am I taking you back to the motel or what?"

"If you wouldn't mind, that'd be great. But I'm just gonna grab my stuff and come back here, but you're right. I'm too tired to drive, especially when I'm still new to the city."

"I don't mind at all."

Wrapping my arm around her waist, I guide her outside. I glance at the cars parked out front, but all I see is the red Corvette that was here last week, my Harley, a Jeep, and an older model sedan. I know the Jeep belongs to Jenny because I've walked her to her vehicle several times, so I start to turn toward the sedan.

Kennedy digs in her heels. "I'm right here," she says, nodding at the Corvette.

My brows shoot up. "You're living in a motel, but you're driving that?"

She stiffens, her body going rigid against mine. "It's the one thing that was all mine, other than the few clothing items and toiletries."

"I'm sorry, I didn't mean to upset you. It's just..."

"You didn't think someone like me would own something like that."

Now it's my turn to go rigid, and I twist to look at her. "Don't put words into my mouth," I growl. "All I meant was that you aren't a flashy girl, and that's a flashy car."

"How do you know I'm not flashy?"

I take a step back and let my eyes travel the length of her body. When I look at her face again, I smirk. "Kennedy, you're wearing jeans, a hoodie, and sensible tennis shoes. There's nothing flashy about that."

"Fair enough," she acquiesces. She pulls a set of keys out of her purse and hands them to me. "Let's just go."

I open the passenger door for her, then walk around to the driver's side. After sliding my large frame into the small sports car, with a few giggles from her, I turn on the engine.

"Her name is Ruby."

"You named your car?"

"I did."

"Fuck, you just keep getting better and better."

Kennedy shakes her head. After she gives me the name of the motel, I pull away from the curb and head that way. Traffic is almost non-existent at this hour, so I easily navigate the city streets, both of us quiet for several minutes. She's the first to break the silence.

"Would it surprise you to know I spent the majority of the last ten years in designer clothes and evening gowns?"

"Why?"

"Because that's what was expected of me," she says simply. "Between the country club, hosting dinner parties, charity functions, and church events, there wasn't any occasion to wear something less... *perfect*." She sneers the word, like it tastes dirty on her tongue.

"Forgive me for being dense, but didn't you say you were brought up in the church?"

"Yes."

"Now, I get that you didn't specify what church, but last time I checked, most churches frown upon vanity and shit.

How is it that yours had so many stupid fucking expectations?"

"The church I grew up in was different. It's more like a—"

"Cult," I deadpan.

Kennedy doesn't respond right away, instead leaning her head against the seat as if she needs time to choose her words. When she does speak, there's surprise in her tone.

"Yeah, I guess. It was as close to a cult as it could get, I suppose."

"That sucks."

"It really did," she agrees. "Don't get me wrong, I didn't have a terrible life. I just didn't have the life I wanted."

As I drive the rest of the way to the motel, I mull over her words. My childhood wasn't perfect, but my parents didn't shove shit down my throat or force me to believe one way or another. They did their best to raise a good man, and I think they succeeded. Sure, I'm not a law-abiding citizen, and I'm in an MC that engages in activities that would have my mother rolling in her grave, but my heart's in the right place.

Most of the time.

"Room one oh eight," she says when I pull into the motel parking lot.

I park the Corvette and follow her inside. I expect there to be boxes of stuff, but all I see is a duffel bag and a shoe box perched on the small table in the corner. Kennedy makes quick work of shoving her meager belongings into both, and two minutes later, she declares herself ready to go.

It's the one thing that was all mine, other than the few clothing items and toiletries.

She wasn't kidding.

"I just have to check out real quick, and then we can be on our way."

"Okay."

I walk her to the front desk and am shocked when she pulls cash out of the shoebox to pay the balance on her bill. Wanting to reach for my wallet and pay for it myself, I force my hands into my pockets, so I don't offend her again.

Twenty minutes later, I'm parking her vehicle back in front of Barlow's Bar.

"There's a back lot, right?" I ask.

"Yeah, but I don't really want my car back there with all the attacks happening. I'll feel safer getting in and out right here, where there's more light and people."

I nod. "Makes sense. But as long as I'm around, you never have to be scared. I won't let anyone hurt you."

"And you can't be here twenty-four-seven."

No. No, I can't. But still...

"Point taken."

I hand the keys to Kennedy, grab her bag and shoe box, and we head inside. Jenny is still here, despite the bar having been closed for almost an hour.

"You're back," she says when she spots us.

"What are you still doing here?" Kennedy asks.

"I just wanted to make sure you got settled okay." Jenny's gaze slides to me, and she smirks. "But I shoulda known someone else would be taking care of that."

"I... we..." Kennedy stutters.

"What she's trying to say is thank you, but we're good," I say, my lips twitching.

"I'm sure you are."

Jenny reaches under the bar and grabs her purse before striding to the door. "Kennedy, you sure you're still good to cover the security installation tomorrow?"

"Absolutely."

"Okay. I should be here by one, at the latest." She winks. "Have a good night, you two."

And then she's gone, leaving Kennedy practically jumping out of her too-sensible tennis shoes.

"C'mon." I rest my hand on the small of her back. "Let's get you upstairs so you can get some sleep."

Kennedy nods and scurries ahead of me, clearly uncomfortable. I don't know if she's worried I'm going to jump her the moment we get in the apartment or what, but she shouldn't. The more time I spend with her, the more I realize that, regardless of what she says, she's not ready to dive into a life of sin.

She's going to require that patience she asked for, yes. But this situation is delicate, and I need to treat it as such. I don't want to simply teach her my ways.

I want to make her fall in love with them, and me, and not be able to bear the thought of walking away when she's done figuring herself out.

CHAPTER 14
KENNEDY

"So, tell me everything."

Glancing up from the laptop, I shake my head at Jenny. Some of the Satan's Legacy brothers have been here for a few hours, setting up the new security system, but Dip is nowhere in sight, which leaves me feeling empty.

"There's nothing to tell."

"How can there be nothing to tell?" she demands. "When I left, Dip was ready to jump your bones."

"I don't know what to say." I shrug. "He walked me upstairs, kissed me on the cheek, and then left."

"He... No. No, no, no." She turns in a circle as if looking for something. "Where is he?"

I can't stop my laugh at her obvious disappointment. "Don't know. He didn't come with the others this morning."

Jenny huffs out a breath as she tosses her purse onto the bar and digs through it. When she pulls out her cell, unease skates through me.

"What are you doing?"

"I'm calling Dip to give him a piece of my mind." I lunge for her phone, but she ducks out of the way as she dials and puts it to her ear. "Hey, Dip," she says, so I know he answered. "Where the fuck are you?" Her scowl slips. "Oh, well... okay." Jenny darts her eyes to me. "Yeah, she's here, but no, you can't talk to her. Call her yourself if you want to."

She disconnects the call and shoves her phone into her back pocket. My phone rings before I even have a chance to ask her what he said.

I don't recognize the number on the screen, so I ignore the call. My parents have been calling nonstop since I didn't show up to their stupid matchmaking dinner, and it would be just like them to call from a friend's phone to force me to answer.

As I'm setting my cell down, it pings with a notification. I flip it back over and see a text notification from the same unknown number.

Huh. My parents don't text.

I tap on the notification, and my lips curve into a smile.

Unknown: Hey gorgeous. It's Dip. Answer the phone

A second later, my phone rings again, and I answer it this time.

"Hi, Dip."

"Mornin'."

"It's afternoon."

"Yeah, well, I didn't get to say good morning this morning so... mornin'."

"I thought you were going to be here for the installation."

As soon as the words are out of my mouth, I want to call

them back. I told myself it didn't matter that he wasn't here, but apparently, it does.

Dip chuckles. "Miss me already?"

"No," I insist.

"Whatever you say. And I'll be there soon. Something came up at the clubhouse that I had to handle."

"What?"

"I wish I could tell ya, but I can't. Club business."

I have no idea what that means. "Oh, okay."

"What's he saying?" Jenny says, not all that quietly. "Put it on speaker so I can hear."

"She knows I can hear her, right?" Dip asks. "Might as well put me on speaker. That way I only have to say this once."

I switch to the speakerphone and hold the cell between Jenny and me. "Go ahead," I tell him.

"There are going to be times when I can't tell you things or that my plans change, and it's not because I'm trying to hide anything from you, but club business is club business."

"Sorta like church business was church business," I snark.

"It's nothing like that," he snarls. "The secrets we keep are to protect you, and us. They're not because we like hiding things or want to control you."

"I've watched SOA, I get it," Jenny says.

"That's a fucking TV show, not real life," Dip snaps, but then he sighs.

"Well, I haven't seen it, so I don't get it."

"Kennedy, this is one of those times I'm gonna need you to just trust me, okay?"

I stare at Jenny, silently begging for her opinion, and she nods.

"Fine," I say.

"Good. Now that that's settled," Dip begins. "I'll be there soon. Are you working tonight?"

Again, I glance at Jenny, and she shakes her head.

"No."

"Then be ready to go in thirty."

Dip disconnects the call, leaving me to wonder what he has planned. But before I can put much thought into it, the door to Barlow's flies open, and a bartender I recognize from my first night here storms in.

"What the fuck's with all the Harleys out front?" he demands as he stomps his way toward Jenny.

"Why are you here, Bryce?" she asks. "Didn't you get my voicemails?"

"The ones where you fired me? Yeah, I got 'em."

"Then again, why are you here?"

Two of the bikers—Toga and Brady, as they introduced themselves—who are working on the security system amble from the kitchen and zero their attention on Bryce. They don't intervene, but it's clear they're watching and listening.

"Because I work here," Bryce insists. "You can't fire me over voicemail."

Jenny bristles and stabs a finger at Bryce's chest. "You don't work here because I *did* fire you over voicemail. You never showed up for inventory yesterday which left me in a jam. Fortunately, I found a replacement." She hitches her thumb over her shoulder at me.

"Well, I'm here now. So you don't need a replacement."

"Are you really that stupid?" I ask, unable to bite my tongue any longer. Jenny hired me to be the assistant manager so I'm damn well going to assist.

"Excuse me?" Bryce seethes as he steps around Jenny to move closer to me. His eyes are bloodshot, and his pupils are no bigger than the head of a pin. "Who the fuck are you, you stupid bitch?"

"I'm neither stupid nor a bitch," I say calmly, although I'm anything but. Bryce is clearly unhinged, or high, and he's scaring me. But I'm not the weak woman I was raised to be. *I hope.* "My name is Kennedy, and I'm the assistant manager of Barlow's Bar."

Without warning, Bryce hauls his arm back and rams his fist into my cheek. Pain explodes in my face a split second before shooting up my arms when I try to brace my fall. Chaos erupts around me as Toga and Brady jump over the bar to tackle Bryce, and Jenny rushes to my side.

"Oh my God, are you okay?" she asks, running her hands over my body as if assessing for injuries.

I try to open my mouth to speak, but it hurts, so I keep my lips pressed together and shake my head.

"You good?" Brady yells.

Bryce is shouting, demanding to be let go, but Brady and Toga are having none of it.

"I've got her," Jenny assures them. "Just get him the fuck outta here."

"No can do," Toga says apologetically. "Dip's gonna want a piece of this prick for hitting his girl, but we'll keep him under wraps until D gets here."

His girl?

"Fine, whatever, just..." Jenny shakes her head. "Take him to the other corner so I don't have to hear him breathe, otherwise there won't be anything left of him when Dip gets here."

"You can't do this!" Bryce shouts. "I'll have you arrested for kidnapping."

"Dude, shut up," Brady says before elbowing him in the face, knocking Bryce out cold.

They drag Bryce's limp body to the corner and toss him to the floor. I expect them to return to what they were doing, but instead, they stand like sentries, guarding the unconscious man.

"Let's get you some ice," Jenny says as she helps me to my feet. "I think you should probably go to the ER too, just to make sure nothing is broken."

I shake my head, still not trusting my pain level to speak. I've never been struck before. Not by a man or anyone. Dammit, it hurts.

Jenny walks me into the kitchen, where she pulls out a block of ice from the freezer and wraps it in a dish towel before gently pressing it against my cheek. I hiss at the contact but welcome the numbing cold.

"Kennedy, I am so sorry. I wouldn't have goaded him if I knew that's how he'd react."

Jenny is distraught and blaming herself, and I hate that. It wasn't her fault. I need her to know that.

Trying to ignore the agony, I say, "It's okay. Don't blame yourself."

"It's not okay," she cries.

I reach out to grab her hand, and wince at the sharp twinge when I squeeze her fingers. "Jenny, I'll be fine. Promise."

"Shit, you hurt your arms too, didn't you?"

I shrug, instantly regretting the movement. "A little."

"Screw waiting." She gently wraps an arm around my shoulders and guides me back toward the main area. "I'm taking you to the hospital."

I don't even try to argue because I really am in pain, and I'd rather be sure that nothing is broken than assume and make things worse.

We're halfway across the bar when Dip strolls in, a wide

grin on his face. But when he sees me, his grin disappears, and his eyes glow with murderous intent.

"What the fuck happened?" he demands as he closes the distance between us in three long strides.

"Over here, brother," Toga calls from the corner.

"Who the hell is that?" Dip asks as he stares at Bryce, who's now conscious.

"He's an ex-employee," Jenny explains. "Wasn't too happy about Kennedy replacing him."

"Motherfucker!" Dip rushes to the corner and hauls Bryce to his feet before slamming him against the wall. "Did you hit her, you stupid sonofabitch?"

Bryce shakes his head. "No. Of course, not. I would never hit a chick."

You've got to be kidding me.

Brady smashes his elbow into the side of Bryce's head. "Stop lying," he growls.

Dip shakes him. "I'm only going to ask you one more time... Did. You. Hit. Her?"

Bryce says nothing, and Dip shoves him at Brady. "Take him back to the clubhouse. I'll be there as soon as I can."

"Uh, D," Toga says. "We've only got our bikes."

"Take my Jeep," Jenny says. "You can either bring it back, or I can find a ride and pick it up later."

"You sure?" Dip asks, and she nods. "Thanks."

Brady and Toga drag Bryce through the bar, snagging Jenny's keys as they pass her. Dip returns to my side.

"Did you call the cops?" Dip asks.

"No. Your boys handled it," Jenny informs him. "Besides, figured you'd want to handle it yourself."

"Damn right about that."

"I hate to break this up," I say, my entire skull throbbing. "But I'd like to see a doctor now."

Dip eyes me from head to toe. "Is it just your face that's hurt?"

I shake my head, and black spots dance in my vision. "No. Wrists too, from the fall."

"Goddammit," he mutters as he scoops me up into his arms gently, careful not to jostle me too much. "Jenny, lock up the bar behind us. Spark and Magic are still working on the cameras outside, but I'll tell them to stop for the day. I'll have Little Man come back at four-thirty to help you prep for opening, and he'll work the bar with you tonight."

"I can handle the bar, just go."

"I'm sure you can, but I'll feel better knowing there's someone here with you."

"Shelly's on tonight, so I won't be alone."

"I'm still sending him," Dip insists.

"Fine. Just keep me in the loop. I wanna know how she is."

"I'm right here," I say.

Dip rolls his eyes. "I'll text you later and let you know how she made out."

"Thank you, now go."

Dip carries me outside. He quickly tells his brothers to stop working and head to the clubhouse, but he doesn't go into too much detail. One look at me in his arms and an ice pack on my face, and they get the picture.

After settling me into the passenger seat of the Corvette, Dip hurries around the hood and climbs in. He makes quick work of starting the engine and tearing away from the curb. His jaw is clenched, and his knuckles are white from the death grip he has on the steering wheel.

"What's wrong?" I ask.

I was the one who was punched.

"What's wrong?" he seethes. "What's wrong?!"

"Yeah."

"A man put his hands on you, that's what's wrong," he clips out.

Dip pulls his cell phone out of his vest, cutting off further discussion. He shoots off a quick text before pocketing the device.

"Grace will meet us at the ER entrance," he declares.

"Who's Grace?"

He slides his eyes to me and smirks. It's infuriating, but I'll take that over his rage. "Jealous?"

"No."

"And you said you didn't know how to lie," he taunts.

If my muscles could tense any more, they would. "Who is she?"

Dip sighs. "She's Duck's ol' lady, and she's a nurse."

"Oh."

"She can check you out, and if she thinks you need to see a doc, she'll make sure it's one we can trust."

"Okay."

"On a scale of one to ten, how's your pain level?" he asks.

"I thought Grace was the nurse." When he glares at me, I cave. "A nine with the ice. It's numbed it a little."

Dip nods slightly. "I'm sorry I wasn't there."

"It's not your fault, Dip. Just like it wasn't Jenny's. I pissed Bryce off, he hit me, end of story."

"Not even close to *end of story*," he snarls. "He'll pay for his mistakes, trust me on that."

"Do I even want to know?"

He shrugs. "Probably not."

The sign for the hospital entrance comes into view, and Dip pulls into park. He helps me out of the car before lifting me into his arms again.

"I can walk," I mutter. "He hit me in the face, not my legs."

"Kennedy?"

"What?" I huff out.

"Shut up and let me take care of you."

CHAPTER 15
DIP

"You're gonna have a helluva shiner, but it's not broken."

Air whooshes out of me at Grace's assessment of Kennedy's cheek. When I walked into Barlow's and saw her with an ice pack to her face, I saw red. In that moment, I knew my soul got it right because the thought of her being hurt sent my heart into a freefall.

Grace had requested a doctor because she couldn't tell without x-rays if the bone had actually snapped, but he was only in the room for a few minutes to order the imaging and IV pain medication.

"Thas good," Kennedy slurs, the pain meds kicking in.

"The doctor wants to keep her overnight because he's concerned about a concussion," Grace explains, and when I glare, she holds her hand up. "But when I reminded him that we have Carnie at the clubhouse, he agreed to discharge her after a few hours."

"Carnie?"

I brush the hair out of Kennedy's face and smile.

"Carnie is a brother. He's also the club doctor and can monitor you."

"'Kay."

Grace tips her head and studies Kennedy. "This is her, right? The girl you were all gushing about the other day when Sami and I caught you talking about men's fantasies?"

"Thas me," Kennedy singsongs. "Fan-fan..." She throws her arms up in annoyance. "Fancy girl," she says, unable to pronounce fantasy.

I chuckle. "Yeah, this is her."

"You are so screwed, you know that, right?"

"Dip says I won't leaf," Kennedy informs her. "Says he..."

Her eyes drift closed, the medication finally knocking her out.

Grace arches a brow. "You won't leaf?"

I smile, remembering what I told Kennedy when she first asked for my help. "I told her leaving me would make her feel empty."

"Damn, Dip." Grace grins. "I didn't know you had it in you." She checks Kennedy's IV one last time before moving toward the door. "I'll be back in a bit to check on her."

"Thanks, Grace."

"Anything for family."

And just like that, Kennedy is family. Fuck, I love my life and my club.

I wake Kennedy up every thirty minutes for the next two hours. She responds to my questions but falls back to sleep quickly. Ten minutes after that, Grace returns.

"How's the patient?"

"Tired."

"It's the meds. Have you been waking her up regularly?"

"I know how to handle someone with a concussion, Grace."

"I know. Wouldn't have left you alone to do it if I thought otherwise." She starts to remove Kennedy's IV. "As soon as she wakes up and stays awake for longer than a few minutes, you can take her home."

"Okay. Thanks again."

"No problem."

Two hours later, I'm carrying Kennedy into my cabin, against her very crabby protests, and helping her get settled in my bed.

"I wanna go home," she grumps as I pull the blanket over her.

"And you will... tomorrow. Doctor's orders."

I pull the bottle of pain pills out of my pocket and tap one into my palm to hand her. "I'll grab you some water so you can take that." I rush into the attached bath and fill a Dixie cup with water from the tap before returning to her. "Here."

She takes the cup and washes the pill down with a grimace. "Damn, that hurts."

"I know. But the pain meds should help. For now, why don't you try to get some sleep? I've gotta run to the clubhouse to handle business, but I won't be gone long. Maybe we can watch a movie tonight or something, if you're feeling up to it."

"Business?"

"Bryce," I clarify.

"Okay." She snuggles into the blanket. "Wake me when you get back."

"No more arguments?"

"No point."

Leaning over, I press a kiss on her forehead and then

leave the room, pulling the door shut behind me. I haul ass to the shed in the woods at the back of the compound, rage fueling my every step. As I go, I send a quick text to Sami, asking her to go and sit with Kennedy until I get back.

"'Bout time you got here," Magic states when I walk through the clearing of trees. "I don't like having to wait to dole out punishment."

"I know, but he's mine," I snarl as I lift the wooden latch barricading Bryce in his death chamber.

When I push the door open, the stench of piss and fear immediately assaults my senses.

"Jesus fucking Christ," I mutter. "You couldn't hold it?"

"Let me outta here," Bryce demands, more confidence in his voice than there should be for a man hanging from chains bolted to the ceiling. "If you let me go, I won't tell nobody."

"Apparently torture chambers scare proper grammar right out of a guy," Magic quips.

"T-torture chamber?" Bryce stutters with wide eyes, all confidence disappearing.

I glance at Magic and point to the chains. "I don't think he got the memo. Maybe we need to step up our game."

"As you so helpfully pointed out, he's yours," Magic says casually as he leans against the wall. "So, what do you have in mind?"

I shift my stare to Bryce and tilt my head as if studying him. "I don't know. Whaddya say, Bryce? How should we torture you?"

"You shouldn't!" he wails. "Don't torture me. You don't have to. I swear, I've learn—"

I whirl around and deliver a roundhouse kick to his gut, and he grunts with the force. Watching as he swings from the chains, I grin. Damn it feels good to hurt someone.

"The time for groveling is over," I snarl when he stops swaying. "You've got two choices, Bryce. One, you can tell me how you think I should torture you which gives you some control over your death. Or two, I can do whatever twisted shit comes to mind and send you to meet your maker however I see fit." I shrug. "Doesn't make a difference to me."

"I-I don't kn-know," he stutters.

"Twisted shit it is then."

I stroll to the wall where all of our instruments are kept. After looking through them all, I decide on the pickaxe. When I lift the T-shaped weapon from its hook, Bryce's whimpers fill the shed, and I laugh maniacally.

Turning around, I plaster a shit-eating grin on my face. "So, Bryce, you like to hit women?"

He shakes his head, and I stalk toward him, the pickaxe dangling from my hand.

"Yet you hit Kennedy," I say. "Why?" When he doesn't respond, I shout, "Answer me!"

"B-because she took my job," he whines.

I lift the pickaxe and swing it, sending the pointed metal end to pierce his thigh. Bryce screams in agony, his shrieks going straight to the dark parts of me that thrive on violence.

When I yank the pickaxe out of his flesh, blood gushes from his leg, telling me I hit his femoral artery. I would've preferred to drag this out, but no such luck.

"Looks like our time is up," I seethe. "Pity. I was looking forward to hurting you some more."

Bryce's head starts to loll to the side as he struggles to stay conscious. "P-please," he slurs. "Help."

I step up to him and grab a fistful of his shirt to spin him around. "Oh, I'll help you all right."

Glancing at the weapon, I make sure the bloody pointed end is directed at his back, and then I thrust it between his shoulder blades. When death finally takes him, it's not nearly as satisfying as I'd hoped.

"That's your version of twisted?" Magic taunts as he pushes off the wall.

"Didn't mean to hit his fucking artery," I snarl. "I hate when shit goes wrong."

"He's dead, so..." He shrugs. "Not sure how wrong it went. Other than I didn't get to have any fun."

"Yeah, well..."

I yank the ax out of Bryce's back and toss it on the floor. Once a weapon is used, we dispose of it with the body and replace it with a fresh one. That way, if anyone ever comes looking, all they find is a bare-bones hunting shed.

"Go back home," Magic instructs. "I'll deal with this."

My adrenaline is waning, so I do as I'm told. Besides, I want to get back to Kennedy. Now that the threat—if you could call it that—is eliminated, I need to be with her.

Despite the bone-weary exhaustion settling in, I make it back to my cabin even faster than I made it to the shed. I climb the steps on the front porch, and when I open the door, I hear female laughter.

She's awake.

I wasn't gone that long, so I'm a little surprised, but then I remember I asked Sami to come sit with her.

Aw, shit.

CHAPTER 16
KENNEDY

"I think your jailer is home."

I smile at Sami. When Dip left, I hadn't been asleep, and when I heard the door to his cabin open again, a warm sensation filled my veins. But then a woman stepped into the bedroom, and hope that he was coming back to me fled. Despite my protests and bitchy attitude, I was grateful he wanted to take care of me. It felt good to be on the receiving end of some affection.

Sami apologized profusely for waking me up, but I managed to assure her that she didn't. We've been gabbing like schoolgirls ever since.

The door to the bedroom opens, and there stands my 'jailer'. Dip's covered in blood and still manages to be the sexiest man I've ever laid eyes on. He leans against the door frame and crosses his arms over his chest.

"You look like you're feeling better," he drawls.

"The pain meds took the edge off."

"I guess I should be going," Sami says as she stands from the edge of the king-sized bed. "It was great to meet you, Kennedy. Don't be a stranger."

"She won't."

"I won't."

Dip and I speak simultaneously, and he winks at me.

"Uh huh," Sami trills as she leaves the room.

Dip pushes away from the doorjamb and saunters toward the bed. "So, what'd you guys talk about?"

"Nothing really."

The mattress dips when he sets his knee on it, and when he starts to crawl toward me, my stomach flutters.

"Don't lie to me."

I brace my hands on either side of me and try to scoot back, but my wrists are sprained, and I wince in pain.

"Woman, stop doing shit to hurt yourself," Dip snaps.

"I didn't mean to," I insist. "I forgot."

He arches a brow. "You forgot?"

"Well, the pain meds are working. Isn't that a good thing?" I sass.

"It's a very good thing. And I'm glad to see you can form words on the pills because it wasn't working out so well for you with the IV meds."

I wrinkle my forehead to try and recall my time at the hospital, but it's a blur. "I'll have to take your word for it."

"Now, what were you two talking about?"

Rolling my eyes, I sigh. "We were talking about you."

"Oh yeah? What about me?"

I pretend to yawn. "I'm getting tired, Dip. I think I'd like to take a nap."

"And I think you're dodging the que—"

My phone rings, and Dip climbs off the bed to get my purse from the dresser. I hadn't even known it was there. Rather than bring me the entire bag, he digs through it to find my cell, and then he answers it.

"Hello."

I can't hear who is on the other line, but judging by the way he pulls the cell away from his ear to glare at the screen, I can guess.

Shit.

Dip walks back toward the bed but doesn't hand me the phone. "It's your dad," he informs me. "Do you want to talk to him, or should I handle it?"

What I wouldn't give to let him handle it... but the damage is done now, so I reach out my hand and he gives me the cell.

"Hello, Father," I say.

"Kennedy Marie Hollings Stodge, who was that man?" my father demands.

"He's a friend." And because I'm feeling a wee bit salty, I add, "I just got out of the hospital, and Dip is taking care of me."

Dip grins as he sits next to me on the bed. He wraps an arm around my shoulder and tucks me into his side, silently offering his support.

"Dip?!" my dad practically screeches. "What kind of name is Dip?"

"If he's gonna yell at you, put him on speaker and save your fucking eardrums," Dip says with his mouth against my head.

"Do not put me on speakerphone, Kennedy Marie," Father demands.

I do, indeed, put him on speaker.

"Father, did you need something?" I ask.

As much as I hate the man, I'd rather not fight with him. All it does is give me a headache, and I've got one of those already.

"Where are you?"

"I'm in Denver, Colorado," I answer honestly. It was

never my intention to hide from anyone. I just didn't want to be bothered.

"She's actually at my house, sir," Dip adds, very unhelpfully. "Well, more specifically, she's on our club's compound, where my house is located."

I elbow Dip in the ribs, and he laughs.

"Kennedy, are you in danger," Father barks. I get a mental image of him bristling with indignation, and it makes me chuckle. "If you're in danger, I can help you."

"I'm not interested in your brand of help," I remark dryly.

"What's that supposed to mean?"

"Father, you tried to set me up with a man less than twenty-four hours after I buried my husband. All you care about is marrying me off again so that the church doesn't excommunicate you for having a disobedient daughter."

"I fail to see the problem with that."

"You would," Dip snorts.

"Would you please take me off speaker?"

"No, I won't. But I will end the call. Goodbye, Father."

I hang up and toss my phone toward the end of the bed.

"Well, he's friendly," Dip says conversationally.

Now it's my turn to snort. "He's a self-righteous jerk."

"Did your parents really try to set you up the day after your husband's funeral?"

"Yep."

"That's cold."

"That's the life I had."

"You're right, it's the one you had," he agrees. "But it's not the one you're making."

I smile. "No, it's not."

"Do you have any idea how hard it is to have you in my bed and not get you naked?" he asks.

Maybe it's the pain pills or maybe it's just Dip, but his question has my head swimming.

C'mon, Kennedy. It's the life you had, not the one you're making. Soak up what he's agreed to give you.

"What's stopping you?" I counter, feeling brazen.

Dip growls as he shifts me to sit between his legs, my back to his front. "I'm stopping me. You were punched in the face today, given pain medication, and potentially have a concussion. There will be no sexy shit going on in this bed tonight."

"What about tomorrow?"

"Woman, you're gonna make me crazy," he rasps. "We'll cross that bridge when we come to it."

"Okay."

"Now, are you game for some Netflix? Or would you rather I leave you alone so you can rest?"

"You'd really leave me alone if I asked you to?"

He huffs out a laugh. "I'm pretty sure I'd do anything you asked me to."

"Oh. Well, I don't want you to leave me alone. But I do have one request before we find something to watch."

"What's that?"

"Can you please go change out of those bloody clothes?"

CHAPTER 17
DIP

Hot water beats down on my head as I wash my hair. I'd completely forgotten about Bryce's blood all over my clothes when I got back to my place and felt terrible when she reminded me. I'd hopped out of the bed so fast, I probably left her head spinning. I could've just changed, but decided a shower was in order if she was going to be sleeping in my bed tonight.

Done with my hair, I reach for the bar of soap.

Shit. I didn't even offer her a chan—

The door to the bathroom slowly opens, and Kennedy pokes her head around the barrier. I smile when I see her eyes are squeezed shut.

"Dip?"

"Yeah?"

"I, um... Do you think..." She groans. "Can I get in there with you?"

The soap slips from my hand, thudding on the tile, and my cock springs to life at the faint hint of need in her tone.

"Or I can get in after you," she rushes to add when I

don't reply. "I just thought, with a concussion, it might not be a good—"

"Kennedy?"

"What?"

I turn the shower off and step out of the stall, completely uncaring of the water dripping on the floor, and close the distance between us.

"If you can't even open your eyes, how are you going to get in the shower with me?" I ask when I'm less than a foot away from her.

Kennedy startles when I speak and puts a hand on her chest. I reach out and wrap my wet hand around hers before bringing it to my lips and kissing her palm.

"Open your eyes, Kennedy," I demand.

She hesitates, but when her lids finally lift, her beautiful caramel eyes widen as she gasps.

"You're..." She swallows audibly.

"Naked," I finish for her.

"No. I mean, yes, but not. You're covered in tattoos," she says with awe.

I pull her farther into the bathroom and push the door closed. Then I step back and let Kennedy take in my ink. The way she looks at my body has my dick standing at attention, but this is her show, not mine.

Kennedy trails her fingers over the skull on my left pec, then moves to the flag on the other side. Her eyes darken the more she explores, and it's all I can do not to strip her out of her own clothes and give my own inspection of what she's hiding beneath them.

"Like what you see?" I ask when the silence stretches out.

"Very much."

She circles me and traces the Satan's Legacy MC emblem that spans the entire expanse of my back.

"This is the same thing that's on the back of your vest, isn't it?"

"Cut," I correct. "The vest is called a cut. And yes, it's the same."

"It's beautiful."

"Do you have any tattoos?" I ask.

Immediately, I want to kick myself. Of course, she doesn't.

"No, but I'd like one," she admits.

"Really?" I turn around to face her. "Any idea what you'd get?"

She shrugs. "I don't know. Something colorful." Kennedy lifts her eyes to mine. "I have a confession to make."

"That doesn't sound good."

"I'm not worried about showering alone."

"Okay."

"I'm a nurse, Dip. I know I don't have a concussion."

"You're a nurse?"

"Well, I have a nursing degree. The only healthcare I've ever done was when Michael needed me to care for him through his lung cancer. But I know the signs of a concussion, and I've had one before. I don't have one now."

"Then why'd you come in here?"

"Because I thought you were just gonna change, but then the shower turned on." She turns her head away, but I lightly grab her chin and force her to face me. She heaves a sigh. "Sorry, I'm not used to this."

"I know. And it's lesson number one for your new life. No more hiding from me. I can't stand it."

"I'm sorry."

"Lesson number two... Don't apologize for shit like that. I'm not mad, and there's no reason to be sorry. But if you want to figure out who you are, you need to own whoever that turns out to be. Own your shit, Kennedy. There's nothing wrong with that."

"I'm..." She catches herself and smiles shyly. "Okay. I'll work on it."

"Thank you. Now, you were talking about the shower turning on," I remind her, trying to get back on topic.

"Right, the shower. I've always thought showering with a man would be fun."

"Fun?"

"Yeah. I mean... Shit, why is this so hard? I don't even know what I'm doing. All I know is I imagined you naked in here, and then I was opening the stupid door because I wanted to see you for real and not in my head."

So much for taking things slow or being a damn gentleman.

My lips curve into a grin. "Kennedy?"

"What?" she groans.

"I'm gonna take your clothes off now."

Her eyes widen, but she nods.

I brush her hair off her cheek and frown at the swelling and bruising Bryce left on her. If I could kill him again, I would.

Gripping the bottom hem of her sweatshirt, I slowly peel it up and over her head. Her tits are high and firm, but they're hidden from my view by a very sensible, yet sexy, black bra. Next, I unsnap her jeans and push them over her hips, revealing a pair of panties that are equally as sexy, but clearly more about comfort than seduction.

"I... I never needed anything nicer than these," she whispers as she tries to cover herself.

"They're perfect," I rasp, pushing her hands out of my way.

And they are simply because they're on her. She could wear a fucking paper bag and still look incredible.

Reaching around to her back, I deftly unclasp the bra before slipping the straps from her shoulders and letting it fall to the floor. Rather than go straight for her panties, I wrap my arms around her and feel the weight of her breasts against my chest.

"Fucking perfect," I growl into her ear.

Her hands settle on my hips, but she digs her nails into my flesh as my breath skates across her skin. With her still pressed against me, I reach between us and push her panties over her hips, and when they slide down her legs, she kicks them off.

I trail a fingertip from her stomach, up between the valley of her breasts, and lift her chin so she's looking into my eyes.

"Ready for that shower?" I ask.

Kennedy whimpers.

With her hand in mine, I lead her into the shower stall. I adjust the water until it's warm and guide her under the spray. She moans appreciatively and lets her head fall back, and her eyes slide closed.

My eyes are trained on the column of her throat. My cock demands I lower them to take in her pussy, but my brain forces them to remain where they are.

"This feels so good," she says.

"Mmmm."

I watch each drop of water slide down her creamy skin and lean forward to lick at them with my tongue. Kennedy flinches, but I don't stop because she doesn't pull away. Instead, she leans into me, resting her hands on my chest.

I kiss along her collarbone, and palm her tits, flicking my thumbs across her peaked nipples. She moans as she rolls her head to the side, giving me better access. Swirling my tongue around her flesh, I mimic what my thumbs are doing, teasing her senses and driving myself mad with desire.

Moving my mouth to her jaw, I pinch her nipples, and she gasps.

"You like this?" I whisper in her ear.

"V-very much."

I capture her mouth with mine, and Kennedy eagerly welcomes me in. For someone who has minimal experience, she sure can fucking kiss. Our tongues duel for dominance, and I slide one hand to her throat. I don't squeeze or apply any pressure. I just hold her steady, keep her in my clutches.

When I'm certain I'll stop breathing, I pull away and move my mouth to a nipple and swirl my tongue around it. Kennedy grabs my hips and yanks me closer, so close my dick is trapped between us. She grinds her pelvis against me, chasing something she's never even felt before.

"Oh, God," she moans. "Wh-what's happening?"

"Just ride it out," I encourage, then shift to the other nipple. "Ride it out and enjoy."

"B-but..." She throws her head back. "It's t-too much."

"Don't you want me to stop?"

"Fuck no," she snaps breathlessly.

I chuckle against her, and the vibration against her peak is all it takes to send her over the edge.

"D-Dip... Oh, shit..."

"That's it, baby," I croon, close to coming myself just from hearing her moans of pleasure. I wrap my cock in my hand and start to jack off, desperately needing my own release. "I'm gonna come with you," I growl.

It's embarrassing how quickly I detonate, but fireworks go off in my head as my orgasm tears through me.

When we're both sated, I guide her to the corner seat in the shower. I wash her legs and everything in between before moving to her torso, her breasts, and then her hair. Kennedy is like putty, limply allowing me to do my thing, completely unashamed at the intimacy.

"Ready to get out?" I ask when I'm done.

"Mmm."

I lift her into my arms, and she turns the water off as I step out into the bathroom. After setting her on her feet, I grab a clean towel from the rack and dry her off.

"C'mon, sleepyhead. Let's get you some clothes."

I don't bother toweling myself off, choosing to air dry instead, and lead her into the bedroom. After finding a pair of sweats and a t-shirt, I help her dress. I make quick work of changing the sheets on the bed, since I got blood on it earlier, and then I urge her under the blankets.

"Aren't you coming?" she asks when I walk back to my dresser.

"Yeah. Just gonna throw some shorts on and make us some sandwiches." I return to the bed and grab the remote off the nightstand. "Turn on the TV and find us something to watch, okay?"

"Okay."

While I'm making us each a grilled cheese sandwich, I text Jenny.

Me: Nothing is broken. She's staying at my place tonight though.

Jenny: Oh thank God. I thought you forgot about me.

Me: Nope. Just been a long day. How's Little Man doing?

Jenny: I'm keeping him.

I throw my head back and laugh. Little Man *is* damn good behind a bar, but I can't help but wonder if she means for work or pleasure.

Me: Just make sure he comes back to the club

Jenny: Nope. He's mine.

Rather than respond, I tuck my phone into the pocket of my shorts and put the grilled cheeses on a plate. Carrying them back to my room, I can't stop my smile from spreading. Little Man's a good dude, and Jenny's a great girl. Maybe I won't be the only one fucked in the love department.

Love?

Shaking my head, I don't even try to fight myself on it. The second I saw Kennedy, I fell for her. I don't know how I knew, but I did.

She's it for me. She's the one.

CHAPTER 18

KENNEDY

"Yay, you're back!"

Jenny runs toward me as if it's been months since we've seen each other instead of days. I get that I haven't been to work in a week, both of us agreeing that it would be better to wait until my bruises faded, but Dip's brought me into Barlow's a few times. Of course, Jenny threatened him with bodily harm if he didn't.

"I'm back," I agree, wrapping her in a hug.

Jenny steps back and glares at Dip, who's standing at my side. "She's mine tonight. You promised."

Dip raises his hands. "I know. But if I leave her here, Little Man is coming with me."

My friend pretends to think it over and finally nods. "Fine. I've decided not to open tonight anyway."

"What?" I ask. "Why?"

"Because you and I are having a girl's night."

"We are?"

"We are. Complete with wine and gossip and movies with hot guys."

"And that's my cue to leave," Dip grumbles. He tugs me

into his chest and kisses me, right there in front of Jenny and Little Man. Not that I'm complaining. When he pulls away, he winks. "Have fun. I'll call you tomorrow."

"Okay."

"Oh, hey, Dip," Little Man calls as he steps out of the kitchen. "We heading back to the clubhouse?"

"Yep. I'm springing you from guard duty."

"Aw, it wasn't so bad."

Little Man walks up to Jenny and wraps his arm around her shoulders. Dip arches a brow, and my mouth drops open.

"Pick you up at seven on Thursday?" Little Man asks Jenny.

"I'll be ready."

He presses a kiss to her cheek before he and Dip leave, and I stare at her incredulously.

"Um... what was that?"

"That was..." Her face falls. "Oh, hell, I don't know."

"Let's go upstairs, and you can tell me all about it," I suggest.

"I'll grab the wine and meet you up there."

I head through the kitchen and up the stairs to my apartment, the one I've only slept in once. It's been really nice staying with Dip, but it feels good to come back to my own space.

When I push open the door, my eyes widen at the sight before me. There are five vases full of different colored roses on the small table. I rush forward and look for a card, smiling when I spot it tucked under one of the vases.

I open the florist's envelope and read the short handwritten note.

Kennedy,

I didn't know if you'd ever experienced the joy of receiving flowers just because but thought you should.

Always, Dip

"Holy shit!"

I whirl around at Jenny's exclamation, tears sliding down my cheeks. I have gotten flowers before, but never *just because.*

"I hope those are happy tears," Jenny says, closing the apartment door behind her. I hand her the note, and she reads it. "Yep, definitely happy tears."

My phone pings, and I reach into my purse to grab it. Glancing at the screen only causes more tears to fall.

Dip: There are thirty roses there. 1 for each year you've lived and a bonus rose for the 1 lifetime left ahead.

"Is that him?" Jenny asks.

I nod as I type out a quick reply.

Me: They're beautiful. Thank you!

Dip: You're welcome. Have a good night Kennedy

"You're blushing," Jenny gushes. "Why are you blushing? What is he saying? I wanna see."

She grabs my hand and turns the phone so she can read the texts. For a nanosecond, I want to stop her, keep Dip's words all to myself, but then I remember that she's my friend, and this is what friends do. They share things.

When I look at her face, her expression is dreamy. "What are you thinking about?" I ask.

"Girl, you've got a hot biker who's sending you roses and texting you sappy shit." She pouts but doesn't look truly sad. "I'm fucking jealous."

Bumping my shoulder into hers, I giggle. "It kinda looked to me like you have a hot biker, too."

Her frown morphs into a grin. "Yeah, well, my hot biker was putting flowers in *your* apartment from *your* hot biker, not giving *me* any of my own."

"So, there is something going on between you and Little Man?!"

Her cheeks flame red, and she shrugs.

"Nope, you can't do that," I say. "You're gonna want me to tell you all about my time at Dip's place which means you have to talk too. What happened?" A thought occurs to me, so I tack on, "Wait a sec... do you care if I maybe invite someone else over for girl's night?"

Jenny grins. "Aw, you're learning," she teases. "I think that'd be great. The more, the merrier."

I send a quick text to Sami, inviting her to join us. She and I spent some time together when I was staying at Dip's, but it was always cut short by Dip or Snow or one of the kids. The other ol' ladies were always busy, so I haven't met them yet, otherwise, I'd invite them as well.

Well, I met Grace at the hospital, but I barely remember her.

Sami responds that she'll be here 'with bells on'. I instruct her to come to the front entrance of Barlow's, and Jenny and I head back downstairs to wait. Thirty minutes later, there's a knock on the door.

"I hope you don't mind," Sami says when I open it for her. "But I brought the others."

She brushes past me, and three more women introduce themselves.

"I'm Fallon," the first one says. "Toga's ol' lady."

"Grace," the second one chirps. "Duck's better half. Glad to see you're feeling better."

"Dip said you took care of me at the hospital." I smile. "Thank you."

"No thanks necessary. It's my job. But even more than that," she says. "It's what we do for family."

"Dip's lucky to have you all."

"She's talking about you," the third woman says as she nudges Grace out of the way and wraps her arms around me. The hug is awkward, but only for a moment. "I'm Laney. Snow's my brother, and Magic's my old man."

"It's nice to meet you."

Once they're all inside, I close and lock the door before turning and smiling at Jenny. "I hope you heard all of that," I say with a chuckle. "Ladies, this is Jenny. She owns Barlow's, so she's my boss and friend."

Introductions out of the way, we all traipse through the kitchen and up to my apartment. I don't have much space up there, but something tells me, with this group, it won't matter.

"Oh my God," Laney remarks when she steps into my small efficiency. "Don't tell me Dip sent those." She points to the roses.

Heat spreads through me. "He did."

"Fuck," Sami groans. "Snow needs to up his game."

"Didn't know Dip had it in him," Fallon states with a grin.

"He's not normally like this?" Jenny asks. "Because I

told him I'd kill him if he hurt Kennedy. And so far, he's been really sweet, but if I'm missing something, I need to know."

Her protectiveness of me is foreign, but very nice.

Laney shakes her head. "No, this isn't normal for him. Don't get me wrong, Dip is great. But I wasn't sure if he'd ever settle down."

"Laney, you're gonna scare the poor girl," Sami chastises before smiling at me. "Dip's never done anything this sweet, but he's a good guy with a big heart, and he really likes you. So, it's not all that surprising really." Her eyes bounce from one woman to the next before landing back on me. "All of our men were a little rough around the edges. We softened them. Like you are with Dip."

"And you," Fallon says, pointing at Jenny. "Little Man can't stop talking about you."

Jenny groans. "I like him so much," she confesses.

Grace puts a hand up.

"Bitch, you don't have to raise your hand like you're in class," Sami teases. "Just spit it out."

"Is no one gonna tell her?" Grace asks quietly.

"Tell who what?" I ask, my interest piqued.

Laney sighs. "Sami told us there was gonna be wine. Pour the booze, and then we can get to the heavy stuff."

Jenny pours wine into the plastic cups that are one of the few cupboards, and when she passes them out, a wave of unease washes over me. I've never served wine in plastic cups before. Only ever crystal wine goblets that had to have cost Michael a small fortune.

"I, uh..." I lower my head. "I'm sorry I don't have anything nicer."

"Girl, what the fuck are you apologizing for?" Sami

demands. "Booze is booze, and none of us give a rat's ass what we're drinking it out of."

I lift my head. "Really?"

"Really," Fallon confirms before gulping down almost half her cup.

I take a small sip of the wine Jenny poured for me, and it's all I can do not to spit it right back out. Wine has never been something I enjoyed, but I don't have the heart to tell Jenny that, so I'll sip on it very slowly. Besides, I still haven't figured out what alcohol I *do* like, so it's not like I can ask her for something else.

"So, back to the whole 'is anyone gonna tell her'," Jenny prompts.

"Oh, right." Laney and Sami exchange a look before they both level their gazes at me. "You've been claimed."

"What?"

"I knew it!"

Jenny's excited exclamation drowns out my question.

"I told you," Jenny says, smacking me on the arm. "That man is so nuts about you, he staked his claim."

"I..." I narrow my eyes. "What does that mean, exactly?"

"It means you're his," Fallon explains. "It means that he will love you forever."

Love?

"It means he'll kill for you, die for you, do anything to make you happy," Sami adds.

Kill? Die?

The thought of Dip dying twists my stomach into knots and sends my heart into overdrive.

"It means if another man so much as looks at you cross-eyed, he better watch out," Grace says, fanning herself. "I, for one, think it's very hot when they get all possessive."

"But..." I chew on my bottom lip. "I'm a widow! My husband just died a few weeks ago."

Silence.

All eyes turn to me, and it's Jenny who breaks the tension.

"That wasn't a marriage, that was an arrangement you were forced into, honey," she says softly. "But none of that matters. The heart wants what the heart wants."

This is all starting to feel very familiar. Dip claiming me, these women telling me it's a good thing. Michael claimed me, and the church, my parents, all told me it was a good thing.

But it wasn't.

"What about what *I* want?" I ask quietly.

"Well, what do you want?" Sami counters.

I mull it over, let the question zigzag through my brain for a moment. And each time it zigs, I force it to zag because the answer flashing at each corner scares me.

Taking a deep breath, I spit out what seems to be the only response.

"Dip. I want Dip."

CHAPTER 19
DIP

"Who are you?"

I smirk at Duck, who's sitting across from me at the table in church. We're meeting to discuss how the new security system and monitoring rotation is going for Barlow's, as well as to make a plan for presenting the entire shebang to other businesses in the city.

Duck glances at Spark. "Do you know who this guy is?" he asks, pointing at me.

"Fucking hell," I snap. "I get that I've been a little preoccupied, but it's not like you haven't seen me at all the last week."

Snow glares at Duck. "Give him a break, D," he says dryly. "He hasn't figured out that work-life balance yet. Besides, you remember what it was like, right? In the beginning, you want to spend all your time with the woman you love."

"In the beginning?" Carnie taunts. "Prez, it's been several years since you and Sami shacked up, and you still spend more time with her than the rest of us."

"Yeah, well..." Snow grins. "Sami can do a lot more for me than all of you jackasses."

Everyone laughs at that but me. Duck's right that I haven't been around as much, and I feel bad about that. But then I remember what Kennedy looks like asleep in my bed, and all guilt vanishes.

Fuck 'em. I want to be with Kennedy... even if it is just to hang out or sleep.

"Please tell me she's at least a freak in the sheets," Brady says. "Because she's nice and all, but a little too girl-next-door for me."

"Let's get shit rolling," I demand, not wanting to discuss sex with Kennedy, or lack thereof.

"No," Duck groans. "You haven't fucked her yet, have you?"

Dammit.

"Not that it's any of your business, but no," I admit.

I glance at Snow, silently begging him to start church so this discussion can end. He stares at me, assessing, watching, and then he gives a curt nod as if he understands.

"What the patch binds together..."

We all recite the club motto, and just like that, I'm off the hook.

"Toga," Snow says as he looks at our enforcer. "Give us an update on the security system at Barlow's."

Initially, Snow said the system was going to be my domain since it was my idea, but after Kennedy was punched in the face, I've been reluctant to do much outside of being with her. He and I discussed it privately, and I'll take it over from Toga now that Kennedy's back at her apartment.

"So far, so good," Toga states. "Although, it's hard to tell if it's the system or Little Man's presence at the bar. There haven't been any problems that we've had to handle. There was a situation out front, some guy hitting on a group of women and not taking the hint that they weren't interested, but there was a cop patrolling the area, and he intervened."

"That must've been a different night than the attack that made the headlines yesterday," Duck says flatly. "Two women held at gunpoint when they were trying to hail a cab. Plenty of witnesses but no one stepped in, so they were dragged into an alley and raped."

"I talked to my buddy at the precinct," Spark begins. "And the running theory is that there were two or more men for that attack. None of the witnesses are talking though, so it'll be a hard one to solve."

"No DNA or anything?" Magic asks.

"It's too early to tell. There weren't condoms left behind, the victims said their attackers wore masks and gloves, so no fingerprints. It's a mess."

"Dammit," Snow barks. "This can't keep happening. My fucking wife was downtown last night. What if it had happened to her?"

Fear curls a fist around my heart and squeezes. Kennedy lives downtown, works downtown. What if it happens to her?

"All of our ol' ladies were," Magic says. "And they're home now, so they're fine."

"That's not the point, and you know it," Snow snaps. He takes a few deep breaths. "Okay, back on track... How's the rotation schedule going? Does it seem to be working out having the monitors for the system in the guard shack at our gate?"

"Yeah," Duck says. "I've talked to all the prospects, and we've all worked a shift, and it's not really any extra work to watch the monitors while we sit there. In fact, the consensus is that it makes the time go a little faster and isn't quite as boring."

"Good. Any proposed changes?" Snow asks. We all shake our heads. "Then do we start talking to other business owners to roll this whole thing out, or should we monitor Barlow's for a bit longer?"

"I think we need to monitor Barlow's for a bit longer," I say. All eyes turn to me, and I shrug. "As awful as it is, until something actually goes down that we need to handle, we can't be sure the system works. I'd hate to roll this out across the city, promising business owners that we can protect them and their customers, and then not be able to deliver on that promise because the system sucks."

And the very selfish part of me wants more time with Kennedy before I have to shift my focus elsewhere.

"I agree with Dip," Brady says. "We've worked hard for the community's trust for so long, it'd be shit for this to blow that all up in our faces."

Snow nods. "All in favor of waiting, say 'aye'."

The ayes have it.

"Let's give it another month, see how things go," Snow begins. "We'll meet once a week to specifically discuss this. Now, any other business?"

"Nope."

"Nah."

"No, Prez."

"No."

"Church adjourned," Snow states before looking at me. "Dip, stick around for a minute. I'd like to talk to you."

"Ooo, somebody's in trouble," Carnie teases.

The others join him in his taunting, but I ignore it. I've

done nothing wrong and am not the least bit worried. When it's just Snow and I left, I stand and face him.

"What's up, Prez?"

"You know they're all just giving you a hard time about Kennedy, right?"

"Yeah."

"So, you really haven't sealed the deal?"

I throw my head back and laugh. "That's what you wanted to talk to me about? Whether or not I'm sleeping with Kennedy?"

"No, not really." He smirks. "But I am curious."

"No, Prez, I haven't slept with her." I tilt my head. "Well, we've slept, but that's it."

"What are you waiting for?"

I heave a sigh. "Prez, she's... I don't know. She's different. Do I want to bury my cock inside her? Absofuckinglutely. But she deserves better than that."

"Isn't she the one who brought sex up in the first place?"

"Yeah." I thrust a hand through my hair. "Look, I get that no one understands, and I'm okay with that. Quite frankly, I don't fucking care if anyone understands. She's the only one who matters." I glance out the window before leveling my gaze at him. "Do you believe in love at first sight?"

"I do."

"I think that's what I'm dealing with. And despite what she says, Kennedy doesn't need me to dominate her or tell her what to do under the guise of teaching her about life. She needs someone who actually gives a damn about her and what she wants. She needs a man who will pay attention to her actions and her words, someone who puts her first."

"She needs you."

"That's what I'm hoping," I say with a grin. "Fuck, that's what I'm hoping."

"Okay, then." He glances thoughtfully toward the door. "Bring her to the party this week, see how she does around everyone. I know you and she are all that matters in the equation, but trust me when I say, her getting along with the brothers makes a difference."

I narrow my eyes. "Does someone have a problem with her? Who said some—"

"Calm down," Snow orders. "No one has a problem with her. In fact, those of us who've met her, really like her. I'm asking this for you. You're a good man, Dip. You deserve a woman who can stand by your side, not follow you around like a student." He shakes his head. "Never mind. This is coming out all wrong."

"Nah, it's fine. I think I get what you're saying," I tell him. "I'm not worried about it, but I get it. I'm taking her out tomorrow so maybe we'll swing by the party after. But I'm leaving it up to her. I want her to stick around, not run screaming," I deadpan.

Snow smirks. "Yeah, I get that."

"So... Is that all you wanted?"

"Pretty much. Just wanted to get a good read on where your head's at."

"My head is on Kennedy. Always on Kennedy."

CHAPTER 20
KENNEDY

"I'll be right there."

Disconnecting the call with Jenny, I flop down onto the bed. I have a date with Dip tonight and absolutely nothing to wear, so I called her and begged for help. I have a few hours before he's due to pick me up, but I'm nervous and have nothing better to do than stress about what I'm going to wear and whether or not tonight will be the night Dip actually makes a move.

For someone who agreed to teach me about sex, he's taking his sweet time to do it.

When Jenny knocks on my door, I open it and drag her across the threshold. She laughs at me as she holds up a bag.

"I come bearing gifts," she quips.

"Thank God," I groan.

"Thank Jenny."

I roll my eyes. "Thank you, Jenny."

She grabs my hand and pulls me toward the bathroom. After handing me the bag, she pushes me inside. "Change and see if it fits before you go thanking me."

I close the door and peek into the bag. Dumping the contents onto the closed toilet lid, I sift through them and notice every item has a tag on it.

Yanking open the door, I glare at her. "Did you just buy all these?"

Jenny shrugs. "I bought them for my date with Little Man, but I've got plenty of things to choose from and want you to have them instead."

"Jenny," I cry. "I can't do that. These are you—"

"You can, and you will. Now go fucking change."

Sighing, I close the bathroom door and do as instructed. Jenny thought of everything. There's a green lace bra and panty set, both in my size. The jeans fit me perfectly, almost like a second skin, and the black top with silver threaded throughout conforms to my curves. The black leather jacket is short, barely skimming the waist of the jeans, and the tall black boots add a few inches of height.

I glance in the mirror, grinning at the woman staring back at me. I look... sexy. I'm not a vain person, but I've always been happy with my appearance. It just never felt right showing it off in sleek evening gowns and designer suits. But this... this look feels amazing.

It feels like me.

Opening the bathroom door, I rush toward Jenny and throw my arms around her neck.

"Thank you," I say, sniffling.

She hugs me back, but then steps away and takes in the outfit. "He's not gonna know what hit him." She grins. "I'll be surprised if you two make it out of the apartment at all."

My smile widens, but before I can get any words out, my cell phone pings. I grab it from the table and see the text from Dip.

Dip: Can't wait to see you

"I'm gonna head out," Jenny says. "I still have to get ready for my date with Little Man."

"Thank you again, so much, Jenny."

"Anytime, honey. That's what friends are for."

"Have fun tonight."

She bobs her eyebrows. "You too."

And then she's gone so I reply to Dip.

Me: Can't wait to see you too

For the next hour, we text back and forth. He's flirty and fun, and I fall for him a little more with each word he sends.

When I first left Rhode Island, I had nothing in mind but getting away from all the bullshit and starting over. Then I saw Dip and without even realizing it, everything changed. He's made it pretty clear that he wants whatever is between us to be real, to be long term. I'm hesitant, but then again...

What if you find exactly what you never knew you wanted?

I wasn't looking for Dip. I was looking for me. And he's helping me find the woman I am, the woman I want to be.

And I want to be her... with him.

The last hour goes by quickly as I apply my makeup and curl my hair. After one last glance in the mirror, I stroll out of the apartment and head downstairs to wait for him in the bar. I'm sure there's some code or rule that says a man should come to your door, but I'm too excited to stay upstairs.

Right on time, I hear the rumble of his motorcycle, and butterflies flit about in my stomach. My excitement morphs into nerves, but not the bad kind.

Rather than wait for him to know—screw the code or rules or whatever—I hurry outside and lock up the bar behind me. When I turn around and see him straddling his Harley at the curb, my breath catches.

Dip is by far the sexiest man I've ever laid eyes on. He's gorgeous when he's naked, but there's something about the way his muscles ripple beneath the cotton of his shirt and the way his cut brings out the danger in his eyes that make my panties damp.

He whistles appreciatively. "Damn, you're beautiful," he growls.

I look down at my outfit and then back to him. "Is this okay? You didn't tell me what we were doing so..."

"It's perfect," he says as he gets off the bike and strides toward me.

Lowering his lips to mine, Dip kisses me as if his life depends on it. He lifts me into his arms and walks me back toward the wall. I wrap my legs around his waist, and he steals my breath.

But it's over too soon.

"There will be more of that later," he drawls. "But for now, I need to be able to ride and keep us both alive."

"O-okay," I say weakly.

I side down his body and stand, but my legs are shaking. Dip steadies me and guides me to the bike.

"Put your feet on the pegs, and keep your legs away from the pipes," he instructs, pointing both out. "And hold on to me." He winks.

"I think I can do that."

He helps me mount up, and when he gets on in front of me, I scoot as close as I can, pressing my chest to his back.

"Holy fuck, I'm screwed," he mutters.

Dip fires up the Harley, revs the engine, and then settles

a hand on my thigh for a brief moment. He pulls away from the curb and instantly, I understand why bikers ride.

It's freeing. The wind, the sights, the sounds... all of it is definitely something I could never tire of experiencing. And doing it with Dip?

It's magic.

CHAPTER 21
DIP

"This isn't at all what I was expecting."

I fold the blanket and tuck it into my saddlebag before facing Kennedy. Taking her on a picnic wasn't my first idea, but it's the one I kept going back to, so I decided to roll with it. And based on the happiness in her eyes, I'm glad I did.

"I hope that's a good thing," I tease.

"It is." She turns to stare at the mountains in the distance. The sun set a while ago, and the moon casts a faint light, illuminating the peaks. "It's so beautiful here."

I can't take my eyes off of Kennedy. "Yeah. Most beautiful sight I've ever seen."

"Do we have to go home?" she asks, facing me again. "I'm not ready for the night to end."

"Well, see..." I rub the side of my nose. "It's not over yet."

Her eyes sparkle. "It's not."

"Nope. There's a party at the clubhouse. I thought we could go there for a while."

Her excitement dims briefly, but then she smiles and nods. "Okay. That could be fun."

"You did say you wanted to experience being drunk," I remind her.

"I did." She steps toward me and reaches for my hand. I link my fingers with hers. "But I was sort of hoping..."

Dropping her hand, I frame her face. "What were you hoping?"

"I don't know. Maybe that we'd finally..." She sighs. "I was hoping you'd finally make a move."

I want that more than anything. But... patience.

I smirk. "All good things come to those who wait."

"Fine. But please don't make me wait too long."

I press a kiss to her lips. "I won't."

The ride to the clubhouse is pure torture. Her thighs are squeezing my hips, and she absently rubs her fingers in circles over my abs. My cock is rock fucking hard, and my heart feels like it's going to beat out of my chest.

But we make it... barely.

When we step inside, the smell of weed permeates the air, and the bass from the music is pumping so loud, thinking becomes difficult.

Thinking became difficult the moment you saw Kennedy step out of Barlow's earlier.

"Kennedy!" Sami exclaims from the bar before hopping off her stool and rushing toward us. "I'm so glad you made it!"

"I am too," Kennedy replies, her eyes lighting up.

Whatever reservations she had about the party quickly disappear as she's brought into the fold of my family. She's passed from one ol' lady to the next, then from one brother to the next as everyone greets her.

"Here," Fallon says, thrusting a glass of red wine at her. "I figured you could use a drink."

"Thanks." Kennedy takes it but doesn't drink.

After a few minutes of her still not touching the wine, I lean close to her ear. "Is something wrong with the drink?"

She lifts her eyes to mine and scrunches her nose. "I don't really like wine," she admits.

"Isn't that what you all drank at your girl's night?"

"I didn't really drink any. But I didn't want to make any of them feel bad, so they don't know that."

"Kennedy," I chastise. "Always speak your mind and tell people what you want. There's nothing wrong with that." I pluck the wine glass from her hand and carry it to the bar, my other hand clasping hers to tug her with me. "Now, what do you want to drink?"

"I don't know."

"Beer?"

"Definitely not."

"Okay," I say with a chuckle. "How about you try a few things, and we'll go from there?"

"That works."

I start her off with a shot of Jack Daniels, but she can't even get the whole thing down. We go through this process for five different liquors, each one causing her to pretend to gag. But the sixth try is what does it.

"Oh my God, this is good," she says after downing the shot of Fireball. "Really, really good."

"Fireball it is then." I grin as I grab the whole bottle and lead her toward the couches where the rest of the ol' ladies are. "Ladies, Kennedy just discovered Fireball," I tell them as I hand the bottle to Kennedy. "Help her drink it."

As I make my way back toward the bar, all I hear is

good-natured razzing about how Kennedy is gonna get 'so fucked up' and 'dance her panties off'. It warms my heart to know she's having fun, and by the time the night is over, she'll be able to check an experience or two off her list.

Two hours later, I realize my mistake.

Kennedy shed her leather jacket and boots shortly after her sixth shot, but that was five shots ago. I picked them up from the floor and tucked them behind the bar, so they didn't get ruined. And now I'm sitting on a stool, nursing my fifth beer, and watching her shake her ass to *Country Girl* by Luke Bryan. For someone who's never really let loose, she's sure figured it out.

And I'm not the only one noticing. Fortunately for my brothers, they keep their eyes in their head and their hands to themselves, so they all get to live to see another day.

"What's she got that I don't have?"

I slowly turn to glare at Minnie. "Everything."

Minnie brazenly steps between my legs and grabs my crotch. "Gimme another chance, Dip," she purrs. "I can be everything to you, if you let me."

I open my mouth and reach for her wrist to remove her hand, but she's yanked backward and falls to her ass. Kennedy stands there, sweat glistening across her face, looking like some sort of avenging angel in black.

"What the fuck do you think you're doing?" she seethes as she stand over Minnie, her feet braced on either side of her torso. "Were you propositioning my man?"

Minnie, the stupid bitch, sneers. "He was mine before you showed up."

I shoot to my feet. "I was ne—"

"He might have been yours in the past, but the past is over!" Kennedy shouts.

I take a step toward the women, but a hand stretches across my chest, and I glance to my right to see Laney standing there shaking her head.

"Let her handle it," she says. "If it gets too outta hand, we'll step in. Promise."

"It better not get outta hand," I snarl, but I back off.

"Bitch, you'll never satisfy a man like Dip." Minnie smirks. "Your cunt's too vanilla."

"But I bet it's not as loose as yours," Brady taunts from across the room.

"Shut the fuck up, Brady," Minnie screeches.

Kennedy leans down and goes to grab Minnie's top, but Minnie yanks her off her feet, and they roll around on the floor. It's killing me not to step in, but Kennedy winds up on top, so I hold back.

"If you so much as breathe within ten feet of Dip again," Kennedy snarls. "It'll be the last thing you ever fucking do."

"Fuck you, bitch," Minnie spits.

"No, fuck you and your stanky twat," Kennedy counters. She hauls her arm back and rams her fist into Minnie's face, sending blood spurting from her nose. "Next time, it'll be a boot heel up the ass."

Kennedy shoves off of Minnie and tries to get to her feet, but she sways. The party ground to a halt the moment Kennedy yanked Minnie away from me, and there's a giant circle of spectators formed.

Grace and Fallon step up and make sure Kennedy doesn't fall while Sami and Laney each grab one of Minnie's arms and drag her out of the clubhouse.

As for me, well, I'm too stunned to do anything, but a slap on my back jolts me out of my trance.

"Dude, she's perfect for you."

I glance at Snow and nod. "Yep."

"But she's looking a little green, so you might want to get her home."

I whirl to look at Kennedy and see Fallon and Grace guiding her to a couch. Rushing toward them, I grin.

Definitely checked a few boxes tonight.

"C'mon, Kennedy," I say as I lift her into my arms. "Let's get you tucked in for the night."

"No," she grumbles. "I'm having fun."

"I know, but you're gonna be worshiping the porcelain god before you know it, and I'd—"

"Dip?"

As I carry her out the door and to my place, I watch her carefully. "Yeah, Kennedy?"

"I don't feel s'good."

"I know."

"I don't like Minnie," she complains.

"Neither do I."

We reach my porch, and she latches onto my cut and pulls me close.

"You better not fuck her again."

"No chance of that happening."

Once we're inside, I take her straight to my bedroom.

Kennedy frowns. "I want you to fuck me."

"I will."

"Dip?"

"Yeah?" I ask as I lower her to the mattress.

"I think I'm gonna be sick."

I whirl around with her still in my arms and race into the bathroom. Somehow, I manage to get her on her knees in front of the toilet just as she hurls.

While she pukes up almost an entire bottle of Fireball, and the remaining picnic contents in her stomach, I get a washcloth and run it under cold water. Sitting on the floor, I straddle her from behind and hold her hair out of her face and set the washcloth aside.

"That's it," I croon, rubbing her back lightly. "Get it all up."

I don't know how long she throws up for, but the dry heaving begins and each time her body seizes, mine coils tight. I hate watching her suffer. But I know she has to get it out of her system if there's any hope of her getting some sleep tonight.

When she's finally done, she collapses against me, and I scoot us both back so I can lean on the wall.

"I'm never getting drunk again," she mutters.

I press the washcloth to her forehead and hold her to my chest.

"Everyone says that," I inform her.

"Maybe, but I mean it."

I chuckle. "Everyone says that too."

"Shut up," she snaps, but her tone is laced with exhaustion.

"Okay."

Several minutes pass, and her body goes limp. Kennedy is tiny, so it's easy for me to maneuver and stand with her in my arms. I carry her to bed and lay her down before stripping her out of her sweaty clothes.

I smile at the green lace bra and panties. Damn, she really was trying tonight. I leave those on her, wanting to see them in the light of day and when she's stone cold sober. That way, I can tear them off her body and ravish her the way we both want.

After taking my clothes off and tossing them into the corner, I climb into bed next to Kennedy and pull her close.

She rolls over and wraps an arm around my waist before nuzzling into my chest.

"G'night," she mumbles.

"Night, Kennedy."

Her breathing evens out, and I press a kiss to her head.

"Love you," I whisper.

CHAPTER 22
KENNEDY

Sunlight streams through the windows, and I roll over, only to be met with a solid wall of heat. I try to open my eyes, but pain lances my skull, and I groan.

"Good morning."

My eyes fly open, despite the agony, and I see Dip grinning at me. My senses slowly come to life, making me aware of several things all at once.

One: The cotton sheets feel like heaven against my skin.

Two: I'm in so little clothes that I can feel the sheets.

Three: I can also feel Dip's erection pressing against my stomach.

Four: If I can feel his erection, that means he's naked.

Five: My nipples are hard, and my thighs are clenched.

And six: My head hurts too bad, and my mouth tastes too sour to do a damn thing about any of it.

"What's good about it?" I grumble.

"You're here," he says.

"I think I'm dead."

His smile widens. "That'll pass." He presses a kiss to my lips before sliding out of bed. My eyes zero in on his ass, and an involuntary moan escapes. Dip chuckles. "I'm gonna get you some Tylenol, water, and then you're gonna sleep. If you're feeling up to it later, we can work on more of your lessons."

The idea that sex with him isn't completely off the table today eases some of my frustration, and I pull the blanket over my head. When Dip returns, he tugs it down enough so I can sit up and take the white tablets and wash them down with the water.

"Sleep," he instructs, returning the blanket to block out the light. "I'll be here when you wake up."

The next time I open my eyes, the room is bathed in darkness. I roll over to look out the window and see that Dip closed the blinds. Strips of sunlight squeeze through the tiny slits, but not enough to make my head throb.

Quickly assessing my body, I realize my headache is gone, and I have to pee. I climb out of bed and hurry into the bathroom to do my business. After washing my hands, I spot the toothpaste and an electric toothbrush. I dig around in a drawer to look for a clean head and then change it out so I can brush my teeth and get the vomit taste out of my mouth.

Feeling marginally better, I open the door and freeze.

Dip is standing next to the bed, naked as the day he was born. My now clean mouth waters, and my pussy throbs.

"Feel better?" he asks as he stalks toward me, his cock bobbing in all its glorious hardness as he walks.

I open my mouth to speak, but nothing comes out, so I nod instead.

"Good."

Without warning, Dip hauls me to his chest and slams his mouth down on mine. I jump and wrap my legs around him, and he shifts to brace my back against the wall.

"I'm gonna fuck you," he growls when he rips his lips away. "Do you want me to fuck you, Kennedy?"

"Y-yes."

"When we're done, there will never be another cock that will satisfy you like mine."

"I don't want another cock." I claw at his chest, work my hands over his shoulders and pull his head closer. "I only want you."

"Goddamn," he breathes.

Dip slides his arms under my ass and carries me to the bed. He lays me on the mattress and crawls over my body. Then, as if a light bulb goes off in his head, he twists and reaches for the nightstand. Dip yanks open the drawer so hard, it crashes to the floor.

"Shit," he mutters.

"What are you doing?" I ask.

"Condom," he rasps. "Need to fuck you but need a condom."

"I'm on the pill."

He stills, his gaze level on mine. "What?"

"I'm on the pill." I shrug. "I did what I had to do."

"Oh sweet Jesus," he groans. "Kennedy, I don't know if I can handle fucking you bare. I'll last two damn seconds."

"Then you'll just have to fuck me more than once," I say, pulling him back on top of me.

"I can do that," he says just before settling his lips over mine and thrusting his tongue into my mouth.

His kiss is electric, intoxicating... sinfully wicked. I thought being with a man would be awkward because of my lack of experience. But with Dip, it's as natural as breathing.

Dip trails his tongue across my bottom lip, down over my jaw, licking a path to my nipple before sucking it into his mouth. He drags a fingertip along my side toward my hip, and goosebumps break out over my flesh. When he moves his hand between our bodies and dips a finger into my folds, my hips buck.

He slips a finger inside of me and uses his thumb to press against my clit. I recognize the building heat between my legs, the waves of ecstasy about to crash over me, but before I fly, he withdraws his hand, and my nipple pops out of his mouth.

"No," I cry, tugging his hair.

"Trust me, Kennedy," he rasps as he licks his way down my abdomen to settle his face between my legs. "Just trust me."

Dip flattens his tongue on my clit, and thrusts two fingers between my folds. The onslaught of sensation is almost too much to bear, and I thrash my head from side to side, writhing from the blinding pleasure.

He finger-fucks me as he feasts on my clit, alternating between licking and sucking, never letting up as I ride out wave after wave of my release. Only when my body goes limp does he slow his assault.

"Holy shit," I say with a sigh.

Dip lifts his head and grins at me, his lips glistening with moisture. "We're not even close to done."

He crawls up my body, and I expect him to stop when his cock is flush with my pussy, but he continues until he's holding onto the headboard and straddling my face.

Settling my hands on his hips, I take a deep breath. "I-I've never done this," I admit.

Dip glances down at me. "Look at me, Kennedy." I lift my eyes to his. "If you don't want to suck my cock, that's absolutely fine. All you gotta do is say 'no', and we'll shift gears."

"Do you want me to?" I ask.

He groans. "Yeah, baby, I do. But it's not a requirement."

I hold his stare for a few seconds before glancing at his dick. A bead of precum leaks from the tip, and I do what comes naturally in the moment. I lean forward and lick it off.

"Aw, fuck," he rasps.

Dip's hips jerk, his tip brushing my lips, and I open wide to take him in. I wait for my gag reflex to kick in, but when it doesn't, I close my mouth around him and bob my head.

I have no clue what I'm doing, but judging by the noises coming from Dip, I'm doing it right. I suck his shaft, swirl my tongue around the tip, and when he reaches the back of my throat, I swallow.

"Fuuuuck," he groans as he pulls away and scoots down so his face is level with mine.

Dip lines the head of his cock up with my entrance and thrusts so hard, I see stars. It's not painful, but our joining is primal, frenzied, and the best thing I've ever felt in my life.

He drags his cock back and forth, in and out, lighting up every single one of my nerve endings from the inside out. My body is on fire, and if this is what it feels like to burn, I'll gladly supply the matches.

Dip was right, it doesn't last long, but we both shout our releases to the rooftop, and when he collapses on top of me, I'm nothing more than a puddle of satiated flesh and bone.

Rolling to the side, Dip drags me with him and tucks me under his arm. I rest my head on his chest, savoring the thump of his heartbeat.

"We're going to do that every day for the rest of our lives," he declares. "And twice on Sundays."

Laughter bubbles up my throat, and I snort. "I'm good with that."

Dip lifts my chin with his hand and stares deep into my eyes. "Do you believe me when I say that by the time you feel whole, the thought of ending things with me will leave you feeling very empty?"

I grin at his recitation of what he said to me when I first approached him.

"Yeah. I'm starting to get it."

CHAPTER 23
DIP

ONE WEEK LATER...

"Yo, Dip, anything happenin'?"

I turn away from the monitors and roll my eyes at Little Man. I'm on gate duty for the next five hours, and I'm not thrilled about it. I'd much rather be at Barlow's with Kennedy than sitting here watching her on a stupid monitor.

"Not a damn thing," I tell him. "Where ya headed?"

"I've got a few things to do in the city."

"Would Jenny be one of those things?"

Little Man grins. He's made no secret about dating Kennedy's boss, and things seem to be going well. Every chance he gets, he's no longer hanging out at the clubhouse but in the city with her.

"Maybe."

I shake my head. "Have a good night, man."

"You too," he says, revving his engine. "Hey, you going to see Kennedy later? Maybe the four of us can meet up at the diner or something."

"Yeah, I'm picking her up later. If she's up for it after her shift, I'm in."

"Great, see ya later."

Little Man rides away, and I refocus my attention on the monitors. Kennedy is behind the bar, serving customers, and she's smiling the entire time. She's really come out of her shell and taken to this whole bartending thing. And when she talks about Barlow's there's excitement in her voice.

For the last week, we've been alternating whose place we sleep at, not that much sleeping happens. When I told her I wanted to fuck her every day and twice on Sundays, I meant it. And woman that she is, she's upped her game. We're screwing twice a day and when we get to Sunday, I can only hope it's three times.

The next hour goes by slowly, me staring at the monitors, Kennedy oblivious to my eyes all over her. But then I catch a familiar flash of bitch on the screen from the camera by the door, and my muscles tense.

Minnie is at Barlow's, and she's not alone. I don't recognize the man she's with, but he's muscled and tall, and I immediately have a visceral reaction.

Darting out of the guard shack, I climb on my Harley and fire her up. I pull out my cell and shoot off a quick mass text, knowing someone needs to cover here for me. I include Little Man on the text, despite that not being protocol because he's a prospect. Protocol can go fuck itself as he's probably closer to Barlow's than anyone else.

Me: Trouble at Barlow's... someone cover the gate

Shoving my phone into my cut, I peel away from the compound and race to the city.

What the fuck is Minnie thinking?

She's not, and that's the problem. Minnie never thinks

with anything other than her cunt, and it's going to get her dead. She's already been banned from the clubhouse after what happened at the party, and if I know that vindictive bitch as well as I think I do, she's out for blood. Kennedy destroyed her plans to become an ol' lady.

Kennedy didn't destroy shit. Minnie did that all on her own.

Fifteen minutes and a whole lot of worrying later, I park at the curb in front of Barlow's and hop off my bike. When I step inside, the rumble of another motorcycle drifts through the door, and I glance over my shoulder to see Little Man parking.

"Get the fuck out of here!"

I whirl around and see Kennedy backed up against the shelf behind the bar, Minnie blocking her in. The bitch's *date* is standing behind her, not doing anything, but not stopping it either.

Not that I thought he would.

I shove my way through the crowd, disgusted at the phones pointed in Kennedy's direction. People would rather get a video for social media than help a woman.

"He won't want your rotten snatch when I'm done with you," Minnie snarls.

I launch myself over the bar, and as my feet hit solid ground, I shove the man out of the way before wrapping my arms around Minnie and throwing her to the floor. Knowing Little Man is right behind me, I focus on Kennedy.

Framing her face in my hands, I ask, "Are you okay?"

"Yeah, I'm fine," she responds. "Just a little shaken up." She peeks around me and scowls. "And a little annoyed that no one even tried to step in."

"Get your goddamn hands off me!" Minnie shouts.

I spare her a glance over my shoulder and laugh when I

see Little Man lifting her off the floor and throwing her over his shoulder.

"Take her to the shed and let Magic deal with her," I order. "She's caused enough trouble."

"You got it," Little Man quips as he carries her toward the door.

"My boyfriend will come for you!" Minnie screams.

Boyfriend?

I search for the man he was with, but I don't see him. Somehow, he managed to get away. But we've got his face on camera, so we'll find him.

Returning my attention to Kennedy, I smile. "Why don't you call Jenny and see if she's good with you closing early?"

"No." She shakes her head. "I'm not closing early. The whole scene is over and done. I'm fine."

"Then I'm sticking around until your shift ends."

"Fine." Kennedy stretches her neck and kisses me on the cheek. "Thank you for coming."

"I'll always come, no matter what."

She nods before getting back to work. The chaos dies down, and phones disappear into pockets as customers return to drinking and socializing. I, on the other hand, am a giant mass of chaotic thought.

I don't like knowing that there's a man out there that might want to cause harm to Kennedy. It doesn't sit well with me that she could be in danger.

Isn't that the point of the new security system? Because there's always going to be evil, and you're not always going to be around to stop it.

I shake my head to dislodge the thought, and watch Kennedy work. It takes her a few minutes to settle back into a routine, but by the end of her shift, she's her normal happy self.

Ten minutes before closing, Little Man and Jenny stroll in, and Jenny goes straight for Kennedy while the prospect comes to me.

"Bitch is taken care of," he says.

I nod my appreciation. "Who filled in for me at the gate?"

"Snow was there when I left. I filled him in on what went down, and he thinks Kennedy should stay at the compound for a while."

"Yeah, I've already thought about that." I thrust a hand through my hair. "You still wanting to go to the diner?"

"Sure, if the girls are up for it?"

"If we're up for what?" Kennedy asks, leaning on the bar.

"There's a diner across town," I say. "You ladies hungry?"

Jenny looks at Little Man and grins. "I could eat... again."

"Oh, man, too much info," I complain.

Little Man just chuckles and shakes his head. "Just because you're not—"

"I'm gonna stop you right there, prospect," I snap, smacking him upside the head.

"Yep, got it."

"Do what ya gotta do to close this place down, and let's get outta here," I say.

While I help Kennedy and Jenny clean up, Little Man works to get the last two remaining customers outside and into cabs, both too drunk to drive.

Thirty minutes later, we're all sliding into a booth at the diner.

"So, what's good here?" Kennedy asks, looking at the menu.

"Everything," Little Man says.

"I'm gonna have a burger and fries, with a chocolate milkshake," Jenny expresses.

"Dip, what are you having?" Kennedy leans against me, so I wrap an arm around her shoulders.

"Short stack of pancakes, bacon, sausage, a couple fried eggs, and chocolate milk."

"Seriously?"

"I'm fucking hungry."

"You must be." She giggles. "I don't think I've seen you eat that much before."

"That's because he's too busy feeding on you," Jenny teases.

Kennedy's eyes go wide, and her face flushes. Little Man snickers, Jenny laughs, and I pull back to stare at my girl incredulously.

"Did you..." I grin. "Do you talk about us?"

Kennedy starts to avert her gaze, but when I growl, she sighs and stares me straight in the eyes. "Yes. I do talk about us," she replies, all prim and proper like. "Do you have a problem with that?"

I shake my head. "Nope. As long as it's all good."

"Trust me," Jenny chimes in as she rests her head against Little Man's bicep. "It's all good."

"Do you talk about *us*?" Little Man asks her.

Kennedy snorts. "So much so that *I* know your dick is pierced, and I've never even seen you naked."

Little Man grins and puffs his chest out. "Yep. And I know exactly how to use that piercing too."

"Okay, this has gotten way outta hand," I snap, although there's no heat in my tone because I'm trying too hard not to laugh.

The waitress shows up just then and takes our order.

While we wait for our food, I decide to dive into the conversation I'm dreading.

"Kennedy, I actually wanted to talk to you about what happened tonight at the bar," I say.

"There's nothing to talk about. It happened, it's over."

"And from what I hear, that twatwaffle won't be a problem anymore," Jenny adds.

I glare at Little Man. "I didn't tell her anything I shouldn't, I swear."

Jenny rolls her eyes. "He didn't, Dip. Promise. All he said was she's no longer a problem. I don't know why or how, but I have a brain and can imagine. And good riddance if you ask me."

"Yeah, well, we still have her fucking *boyfriend* to worry about," I explain. "He managed to slip away, and we don't know how big of a threat he is."

"Isn't that what the security system is for?" Kennedy asks.

"It is. But you don't just work at Barlow's. You live there."

"And?"

"And I want you to come stay with me until we find the prick."

She narrows her eyes. "Why?"

I glance at Little Man for help, but he simply shrugs. Jenny isn't worth a damn either because she's grinning like a fool.

"Because I don't want you to be caught alone, and I can't be there all the time. And the thought of you getting hurt sends me into a tailspin," I admit. "I'd just feel better if I knew you were tucked in at night in my bed and not a Harley ride away."

"Okay."

"And the doors and locks on that apa—" I press my lips together as her acceptance registers. "Okay?"

Kennedy shrugs. "Yeah, okay. I'm not all that interested in staying at the apartment anyway. Even if there weren't a threat, I like being at your place. It feels right."

"Just like that?"

"Yep. Just like that."

CHAPTER 24
KENNEDY

"Why don't you come stay with me for a few days?"

Stabbing the speakerphone icon, I set the phone on the counter and start to gather all the ingredients to make dinner. I've been at Dip's for two weeks now, and we've settled into a routine. Too bad it doesn't include me getting to spend a lot of time with him.

Which is why I called Jenny... to vent.

"I don't want to leave." I heave a sigh. "I just miss him when he's not here."

"How are things when he is home?"

"Perfect. He treats me like a queen. But I can tell he's always got a lot on his mind. And it's shit he can't tell me, which is frustrating."

"Yeah, it's the same with Little Man." She pauses. "Although, he's still a prospect so he doesn't know everything. But it's enough to weigh on him at times."

"How are we supposed to handle that?"

"I don't know. Have you talked to the other ol' ladies about it?"

"Yeah. They tell me it's something I'll just have to get used to if I choose to have a life with Dip. They aren't mean about it, but..."

"But?"

"They've been around this life longer than I have, so it's easy for them. I've been around the opposite."

"Yeah, but Laney's the only one who grew up around bikers. The rest of them went through an adjustment period, I'm sure."

"True."

"Talk to Dip tonight, when he gets home. Tell him how you feel, that you're lonely," Jenny suggests. "He wants you to be honest with him, so be honest with him."

"Maybe I will."

"Trust me, Kennedy, you'll feel better after you do."

And it's with that thought in my head that I go about the rest of the day. I spend hours on dinner, setting the table, making everything perfect. But when six o'clock rolls around, the time Dip said he'd be home by, I'm still alone.

The hours tick by, and the food gets cold. I don't bother cleaning it up, choosing to let it sit out so he can see all the hard work I wasted. Maybe it's petty, but I'm pissed. And hurt.

I stop counting the number of times I've looked at my phone to see if I missed a call or text. I haven't.

At one in the morning, I go to bed. But sleep evades me as I toss and turn, the bed and my body feeling too empty.

Four o'clock in the morning rolls around, and still no Dip. Or calls or texts. At seven, I give up trying to sleep and get up.

I work myself into a tizzy, cleaning and doing laundry, but I still don't touch the food on the table. Nope, he's going to see that.

A little after two in the afternoon, the door to his cabin opens, and Dip strolls in. For a moment, I take in the lines of exhaustion on his face, the hard set of his jaw, and want to comfort him. But then I look at the perfectly set table, and my anger ratchets up several notches.

"Where the hell have you been?" I demand, stomping toward him.

Dip's eye twitches, and he glares at me. Silently, he takes off his cut and drapes it over the back of the couch. Next, he peels off his shirt, which is covered in blood, and tosses it on the floor.

"Are you seriously going to ignore me?"

Dip removes his gun from the waistband of his jeans and sets it on the coffee table before kicking off his boots.

"Dip!"

"I've had a long fucking night, Kennedy," he snaps. "I don't need a guilt trip from you."

"Guilt trip?!" I shout. "Guilt trip?! I'll give you a guilt trip, mister." I stab a finger at his now bare chest. "I spent hours preparing dinner yesterday, worked up the courage to have a very difficult conversation with you, and don't even have the decency to call and tell me you won't be home." I take a deep breath before continuing. "You said you'd be home at six, Dip. Six! News flash... you weren't. So I was left here, alone, again, to worry. And I did worry. But I also worked up a pretty good snit, so fuck you for that!"

Dip arches a brow. "Are you fucking done?"

I start to nod, but then shake my head. "No. No, I'm not. I'm lonely, Dip. I'm out here in the middle of nowhere, and when you're not here, I'm lonely."

"Now are you done?"

My body deflates, all my anger dispensed. I nod.

"Fuck me, Kennedy? Fuck me?" he snarls, throwing my words back at me. "I'll show you fuck me."

Dip tears at my clothes. Fabric rips, but I don't care. He's beyond angry, but I know he won't hurt me. There's something about his frantic actions that have me submitting to him, have me letting him take what he needs.

There'll be time enough later to argue.

When I'm naked, Dip yanks me over the end of the couch. "Bend over," he commands, pushing on my back.

The sound of his zipper being lowered sends a bolt of white-hot heat to my core, and I whimper. When his jeans hit the floor, my pussy pulses.

Dip nudges my legs apart and wraps a fist in my hair. "I'm gonna fuck you, Kennedy. And you're gonna be a good fucking girl and take everything I have to give."

"Y-yes."

He thrusts into my wet cunt, burying himself balls-deep, and he fucks me. Dip fucks me hard and fast. There are no more dirty words, no more commands. There's only the moans barreling out of me and the grunts tearing from him.

My pussy clenches around him as my orgasm hits, and he picks up his pace. Dip pounds me from behind, gripping my hips so tightly, I know there'll be handprints when he's done.

And I love every angry second.

Dip thrusts and withdraws, slams in and pulls out, over and over, until he stiffens, and his cock pulses as he spills his release. He collapses on top of me, both of us sweaty messes.

He reaches toward my face and tucks my hair behind my ear. "I'm sorry," he whispers brokenly.

I wiggle beneath him, and he straightens before guiding

me to sit on the couch. Instead of sitting next to one another, he urges me to straddle his lap.

Framing his face with my hands, I give him a quick kiss. "Do you feel better?"

He huffs out a breath. "I don't know how to answer that question without hurting your feelings."

"Honestly, Dip. Answer me honestly."

He sighs. "No, Kennedy, I don't feel better. I feel horrible."

"Why?"

"Because I hurt you. It was an awful night and when I came home and saw you standing there, and then you tore into me..." He shakes his head. "I would never hurt you for anything, you have to believe that."

"I know you wouldn't. And I'm sorry I laid into you. I was angry and hurt and..."

"And what?"

"Believe it or not, you make me feel safe enough, cherished enough to actually speak my mind."

Slowly, he smiles. "I'm glad, Kennedy."

As we hold each other, I rest my head on his shoulder. A few minutes pass quietly, but then he starts to shake, and I realize he's crying.

I don't pull back to look at him, but I can't ignore the pain of his tears.

"Do you want to talk about it?"

CHAPTER 25
DIP

Do you want to talk about it?

Do I?

No. And yes. I know I should. Normally, I'd talk to the guys, but they're all in the same boat as me. I have no clue if they went home and fucked their significant others senseless, but I did.

And that's on me.

I suck in a few deep breaths, giving myself time to compose myself before I look Kennedy in the eyes. When I do sit back, I expect some of the fire from her anger to remain in her dark irises, but there's nothing there but understanding and compassion.

"I can't tell you everything," I remind her.

"I know. Just tell me what you can."

I nod. "We, uh, implemented the security system early throughout the city. At least with the businesses that agreed," I clarify. "After Minnie and that fuck she was with at Barlow's, we figured the sooner the better."

"He's still 'that fuck'?"

"Spark and I have been working hard to figure out who this guy is, but so far, we keep coming up empty."

"You'll find him," she assures me.

"We will, but in the meantime, there are other bad guys that need our attention. And last night, that was made very apparent."

"What happened?"

"Two guys attacked a group of teenage girls," I bite out. "I don't know what the hell their parents were thinking letting them out that late, but they were. We raced like hell to get there, and we caught the guys. But not before..." I clear my throat. "We were too late for one of the girls."

Kennedy gasps, and tears spring to her eyes.

"How the hell are people supposed to feel safe if we can't stop this shit from happening?"

She cups my cheeks. "Dip, you can't stop everything. What you all do is pretty amazing, and I hate it, but the ones you do save, the things you do stop... You have to find a way to be okay with that."

"We'll pay for the girl's funeral. Anonymously, of course. This is eating all of us up. We have a plan, a system, but it's going to take time for people to realize we're not fucking around. You mess with Denver, our women and children, you mess with Satan's Legacy," I snarl.

"What can I do to help you with this?"

"Fuck, Kennedy, you're doing it," I rasp. "I am so sorry I came home like I did. I'm sorry I made you worry. The fact that you're still here, talking to me... that's all I ask. Just know that there are things I see, hell, things I do that make me go a little crazy. All I knew was the club was too late, you were mad, a dead girl's image took up residence in my head, and I needed something good in that moment to make it all disappear."

"Okay," she says quietly. "I can do that. I can be here for you. But please, Dip, promise me you'll try to text me next time. Not because I want to be controlling, but it'll go a long way to easing some of the worry."

"I can do that."

Kennedy slides off my lap to sit next to me. She lifts my hand, stroking the back of mine with her thumb.

"I've got an hour before I have to get ready for work," she says casually.

"Fuck, I forgot you had a shift tonight."

"I'll be fine, Dip. I'm going straight to the bar. Little Man will be there, so I'll make sure he meets me outside and walks me in."

"Promise?"

"Yeah, I promise."

"Yeah, okay. I'd rather go with you, but I've got a few things to take care of here. I'll meet you at Barlow's before it closes, though, okay?"

"Okay."

Groaning, I push up from the couch. "I really do need to get going." I lean over her and press my forehead to hers. "Are we good?"

"We're good."

"Thank fuck." After kissing her, I add, "Text me when you get to the bar."

"I will."

Feeling slightly lighter than when I arrived home, I head to the bedroom to grab clean clothes. I shouldn't bother because a dead man's blood will be soaking them before long, but I have no interest in putting on the clothes with that girl's lifeforce all over them.

As I make my way across the compound, toward the shed, I let her image return to my mind. I latch onto the rage at finding her dead in that alley, her friends screaming for help as her murderers attack them.

But it's Satan's Legacy's turn now. We're the predators, and those assholes are the prey.

When I reach the clearing, Brady and Carnie are standing outside the door. "'Bout time you showed up," Carnie snaps. "Prez said we had to wait for everyone before we could end their miserable lives."

"Who's manning the gate?" I ask, knowing Little Man is at Barlow's.

"Spark volunteered," Brady says.

"Well, then, I'm here. Let's get this party started."

Carnie lifts the latch and opens the door. The men's screams fill my ears, but I tune them out and focus instead on my brothers' taunts.

"I'm gonna slice your balls off and feed them to you, forcing you to chew through your own sac," Magic snarls.

"And I'm gonna slit your throat and fuck your neck with your own dick," Toga seethes.

"You're gonna feel a million times the pain you put that girl through," Prez adds.

We all go round and round, taking turns explaining, in detail, every twisted way we're going to torture them. There isn't a brother in this shed who's not out for vengeance, and we take our time before we get to the real fun.

I have no idea how much time passes before Magic selects the first instrument, but both men have pissed themselves several times, and one of them has vomited. The stench is both horrifying and fury-fueling.

Leaning against the wall, I watch my brothers take turns with different weapons, doling out punishment, bringing them both to the brink of death without letting them slip over that edge. My phone pings with a text notification, but I ignore it, knowing it's probably just Kennedy letting me know she arrived at Barlow's. Within seconds, it starts to ring, but I silence it, eager to begin my turn.

"Dip, you're up," Snow says as he tosses the ice pick to the floor.

Pushing off the wall, I stride toward the weapons, taking my time to pick the most brutal of what's left.

"There's not much breath left in them, Dip," Carnie calls from across the shed. "Might wanna hurry up."

Another cell phone rings as I reach for the machete. I'm dimly aware of Snow answering the call, but I tune him out and spin around to face the men barely clinging to life as they dangle from the ceiling.

"Which one of you wants to go fi—"

"Motherfucker!"

I whirl around to face Snow. "What is it, Prez?" I ask.

"Brady, Carnie, finish this," he orders. "The rest of us are riding to Barlow's."

My stomach bottoms out. "Prez?"

Snow closes the distance between us and grips my shoulders. "Keep your head, Dip."

"What the fuck is going on?"

"That was Jenny. Little Man never made it to the bar." He takes a deep breath and frowns. "Neither did Kennedy."

CHAPTER 26
KENNEDY
TWENTY MINUTES EARLIER...

"Sorry, Kennedy. Not trying to be a dick."

"It's okay, Little Man. Is everything okay at Barlow's?"

"It's fine. Spark texted me on my way here that the camera aimed at the back lot is out, so I've been trying to fix it. And Jenny got a wild hair up her ass to open early, so the place is packed, and I'm stuck outside. I haven't even seen her yet."

I chuckle at his annoyance. It's hard to tell whether he's more upset about not seeing Jenny or the camera, but of which suck I suppose.

"I'll be there soon. I'll park out back so you don't have to stop working and come escort me inside."

"Thanks, Kennedy."

"See ya in a few."

I disconnect the call and stomp on the gas. If Jenny opened early, why didn't she tell me? I would've come in sooner.

Maybe she's too busy.

When I reach Barlow's, I see what Little Man meant.

There are zero empty spaces out front, and several people spill out onto the sidewalk as if there's not enough room inside to enter. I turn down the alley toward the back lot, but when I park the Corvette, I don't see Little Man.

Getting out of the car, I scan the lot, searching for him. He's nowhere in sight. Maybe he went inside to help Jenny, since clearly we're busier than I've ever seen it.

As I walk to the back entrance, I dump my phone and keys into my purse. Just as I reach for the handle, an arm snakes around my neck, and a hand clamps over my mouth.

"Don't even think about screaming," a man whispers against my ear. "Slowly take your keys back out of your purse. We're going upstairs."

He drags me up the steps as I thrash against him and struggle to break free. It's useless though because he's much stronger than me.

"Stop fighting me, you stupid bitch," he snarls as he slams me against the apartment door. "Unlock it," he demands.

I fumble with the key to fit it into the lock, my hands shaking. When it's finally inserted, I twist the knob, and the man shoves me inside, sending me tumbling to the floor. I scramble to my back and lobster-crawl away from him.

"Who are you?" I ask as he slams the door and locks us inside.

And when he turns around, I know. It's Minnie's boyfriend. 'That fuck' has found me.

"I'm the guy who's going to make that biker cunt pay for killing my girlfriend," he barks.

I dart my eyes to the other door, debating on whether or not I could get away from him, but he grabs my arm and drags me to the bed.

"Go ahead and scream," he taunts. "The music is so fucking loud, no one will hear you. I made sure of that."

"What did you do?"

"Social media is great for spreading the word about a party, isn't it?"

"You're why it's so busy?"

"Of course, I am. Barlow's Bar couldn't draw in this many people on its own."

"Where's Little Man?"

"Your biker friend who was working on the camera I broke?"

Bile rises up my throat at the evil grin that spreads across his face.

"Where is he?"

"In the dumpster, where trash belongs."

My heart plummets.

No. No, no, no. Little Man can't be dead.

"And that's where you'll be when I'm done with you." He smirks. "But not before sending your boyfriend something to remember you by."

He grabs a fistful of hair and forces me to my feet before throwing me down on the bed. I try to scramble away, roll off the other side, but he yanks me back by my ankle.

"Ah, ah, ah," he tsks. "Not so fast."

"Why are you doing this?"

He laughs bitterly. "Are you that stupid?" It's a rhetorical question, so I don't respond. "Minnie is dead because of Satan's Legacy. You were the easiest target, so I'm taking my pound of flesh from you."

"If you loved her so much, why was she a whore for the club?"

Shut up, Kennedy! Don't antagonize him.

"She was what she was long before I met her. I didn't

care who she spread her legs for, as long as she came home to me."

Wow.

"Ya wanna know what else?"

"W-what?"

"Your boyfriend fucked my girlfriend, so it's only fair that I get to fuck you." He nods. "Yeah, I'm gonna have a little fun before I kill you."

He starts to unbuckle his belt one-handed, keeping his other hand wrapped around my ankle. When he shoves his pants down, his flaccid penis hangs between his legs like a limp noodle.

Using the leg he's not restraining, I kick him in the balls, and he stumbles backward with a shout.

"Help!" I scream as I get to my feet and try to make a break for it. "Help me!"

"You stupid bitch!" he seethes, yanking me back by my hair and forcing me to the bed again.

He pulls a knife out of his pocket and presses the blade to my throat.

"Do that again and see what happens," he taunts, cutting into my flesh.

Blood trickles down my skin, but I force my mind to ignore it. He takes several lengths of twine out of his other pocket and ties my hands and feet to the bed posts, putting me on display like some sacrificial virgin.

I try to fight him, to kick and punch and scream. But nothing works. All I get for my trouble are more cuts across my chest and rope burns on my wrists and ankles.

After I'm tied up, he starts to jack himself off, I assume in an effort to get it up. I turn my head away and lie perfectly still, praying to a God I fucking hate for Dip to realize I haven't texted him and save me.

CHAPTER 27
DIP

"Answer the phone, dammit!"

I rush toward the main entrance to the compound, dialing Kennedy's number over and over again, only to keep getting no answer.

"Kennedy, call me when you get this," I demand on her voicemail.

"We'll get there in time, brother," Duck says, running in step next to me.

"And if we don't?"

"We don't even know that something is wrong," Snow says. "Maybe she got a flat on the way or something."

"And Little Man?" I demand. "He get a flat too?"

Jenny was who called Snow, pissed off because she was slammed at the bar and Little Man hadn't shown up yet. She was also worried because Kennedy hadn't arrived, and she's never late.

When we reach the gate, Spark is sitting in the guard shack, watching the monitors.

"What's going on at Barlow's?" I demand, hauling him out so I can see for myself.

"Whaddya mean?"

My eyes zero in on the blank screen. "What's wrong with this camera?"

"I dunno," Spark says. "But Little Man is working on it."

"You talked to Little Man?" Snow asks.

"Yeah. I text him about the broken camera, and when he responded, he said he'd just gotten there and would work on it."

"Jenny called and said he never made it."

"Maybe he didn't go inside first?" Spark suggests.

"Kennedy didn't get there either," I snap.

"What?"

"Jenny said neither of them were there."

As we're standing there talking, wasting time, the monitor flashes and suddenly, the camera is working. I stare at the screen, searching for something, anything, to tell me what the fuck is going on, and then I see it.

The lid to the dumpster moves.

"Prez, come look at this," I seethe.

Snow steps into the shack, and I point to the screen.

"There, see that?"

"Is that..."

As we're watching, Little Man appears from beneath the lid and rolls over the edge of the dumpster onto the ground.

"What the fuck?" Prez mumbles as he whips out his phone. Several seconds later, he taps the cell and shoves it back in his pocket. "He's not answering. Let's ride!"

Ride we do. We ride like bats outta Hell, swerving in and out of traffic, ignoring the blaring car horns and middle fingers.

As we race into the city, I cut through alleys and parking lots, familiar with all the fastest ways to get where I need to be. And when I pull into the back lot of Barlow's, I skid to a stop.

"Little Man!" I shout, putting the kickstand down and dismounting to run to him. "Little Man, what the fuck happened?"

"Don't know," he mutters as he tries to sit up, but he can't stay upright without my help. "Was working on the camera and..."

"Where's Kennedy?"

"She's not inside?"

The rest of my brothers pull into the lot, and Snow's off his bike in an instant, striding toward us. "Duck, go inside and check things out. Make sure Kennedy didn't get here while we were on our way." Duck blows past him to do as ordered. "Little Man, brother, are you okay?" Prez asks, kneeling beside him on the pavement.

"Fine. Gotta headache though."

Little Man touches the back of his head and his fingers come away bloody.

"Magic, call Carnie and have him bring the van. I don't want Little Man driving. He needs to be checked out though."

"I'm fine, Prez," Little Man insists, even as he sways.

"No, you're not," Snow snaps.

The back door flies open, and Duck spills out. "Kennedy isn't inside. But I overheard someone talking about a social media post they saw about a party here tonight. I'm guessing that's why it's so busy."

"Motherfucker!" I roar, shooting to my feet.

If there'd been a party, Kennedy would've known about it and told me. I pull out my cell and dial her number again. It rings and rings, and then her voicemail picks up.

"Call her again," Toga orders.

"She's not answer—"

"Call. Her. Again!" he shouts. "And be quiet so I can listen.

Kennedy's phone rings, and Toga takes off toward the back stairs to the apartment.

"I hear it ringing," he shouts.

I hurry after him, barreling past him halfway up the steps. When I reach the small landing, I heave my shoulder into the door, severing it from its hinges.

From this entrance, you can see Kennedy's bed, and standing next to it, buck naked and jacking off, is a man. Kennedy is tied down, her clothes hacked off her body and in shreds, and blood trickles from multiple wounds marking her flesh.

Red hot rage boils in my veins. "Get the fuck away from her!"

I tackle the man, both of us rolling to the floor until I'm straddling him. Recognizing him immediately as Minnie's boyfriend, I deliver punch after punch, crushing blow after crushing blow.

I'm dimly aware of my brothers passing me to tend to Kennedy, aware of her crying and begging for me, but it's as if I'm under water. Nothing makes sense, nothing else matters but erasing this fuck from existence.

"I'm gonna fucking end you," I snarl.

"Dip."

I hear my name but tune it out. My knuckles swell, and my chest heaves, but I don't stop. Rising to my feet, I kick the man in his ribs, his head, his shriveled fucking dick.

Arms wrap around me from behind, and I thrash against them, breaking free to pull the gun out of my waistband and point it at the guy's broken and bashed in face.

"You fucked with the wrong woman," I growl as I

squeeze the trigger, sending a bullet straight between his eyes.

"Dip!"

I take a deep breath before turning to face my president. Snow is standing next to the bed glaring at me, and Duck and Toga are working to untie Kennedy. Magic is tucking a blanket around her in an effort to give her some sense of modesty.

I could've lost her.

All because of the kind of evil the club will never be able to wipe out. I almost lost the love of my life because there are sick people in the world, and sick people very rarely step out into the light.

You could've lost her, but you didn't.

"Dip," Snow prods.

"I..." I shake my head. "What if he'd killed her?"

"Dip," Snow snaps. "She's right fucking here! Alive."

I level my gaze on Kennedy, hating the fear in her eyes. And it's all my fault. I should've been with her, not in the shed wasting my energy on two murderers.

"Dip," Kennedy mewls.

As if snapped back from the jagged edge of oblivion, my feet move, carrying me toward her.

CHAPTER 28

KENNEDY

Shivering, I watch as Dip strides across the small apartment toward me. He was lost for a few minutes, but when he heard my voice, it was like a rubber band snapped him back to reality.

"Can you guys give us a few minutes?" he asks as he kneels on the mattress next to me.

"C'mon," Snow says. "You heard the man."

Toga, Magic, Duck, and Snow leave the apartment just as Jenny and Little Man barrel through the entrance from the kitchen.

"Oh my God," Jenny cries as she rushes toward me. "I didn't... Fuck, I... You..."

Little Man wraps his arms around Jenny and tries to console her. "It's okay, babe. You didn't know."

"He's right," I say. "There's no way you would've known what was going on up here because of the crowd and music, Jenny. It's not your fault." I look at Little Man. "I take it you got the camera fixed."

He shakes his head. "Nope. Was knocked out and tossed

in the dumpster," he says with a scowl. "I'm sorry, Kennedy."

"But the camera *is* working," Dip informs them. "That's how we knew something was wrong. We watched on the monitors back at the compound when you crawled outta the damn trash," he tells the prospect. "I don't know how it started working again or wh—"

"There was a loose wire," Little Man states. "I messed with it and was just about to call Spark to see if it was working again when..." His gaze slides to the dead man. "... he struck."

Dip growls, and I reach for his hand. "It must've taken a while to come back online."

"Probably. Might want to see if we can do anything to make that faster somehow."

"I'll bring it up in church, believe me."

Little Man nods before turning Jenny in his arms so he can look her in the eyes. "Jenny, why don't we go back downstairs and give them some privacy?"

"Um... who's watching the bar?" I ask.

"I shut it down," Little Man says. "You're closed."

I blow out a breath and nod. "Okay."

"Kennedy, are you sure you're gonna be okay?" Jenny asks, looking forlorn.

"I'll be fine, Jenny," I assure her. "I promise."

She nods, and Little Man leads her out of the apartment.

"Finally," Dip mutters.

"Dip, I—"

"I need to know, Kennedy," he rasps.

"Need to know?"

"Did he... What did he do to you?"

"Does it matter?"

Please don't matter.

He shakes his head and leans forward to brush a kiss across my lips. "No, Kennedy. It doesn't matter, not in the sense that it changes anything I feel for you. But I need to know. I just..."

"If I don't tell you, you won't be able to let it go? Is that it?"

"Yeah, baby, that's it."

"He didn't rape me, Dip. He threw me to the floor, cut me up a little, but he didn't rape me."

He releases a long breath, exhaling some of his worry away. Dip shifts so his back is against the wall and pulls me onto his lap.

"I was so scared, Kennedy. When Snow told me you hadn't made it into work..." He swallows. "I can't lose you."

"I'm right here." I link my fingers with his, settling both our hands against my stomach. "I'm here, and I'm okay."

"You're moving in with me," he says flatly.

I smile. "Okay."

"And I want you to quit working here."

"No."

"Excuse me? This job could've cost you your life."

I drop his hand and turn around to straddle his lap. "But it didn't, Dip. I didn't die. And men like him," I say, tipping my head toward *that fuck*. "They won't cease to exist if I stop working here. So, no, I won't stop. I love it here. I love Jenny. Please don't ask me to give up something I finally found for myself."

He arches a brow. "What if I insisted?"

"Do you really want to test that theory?"

Dip heaves a sigh. "No. And for the record, I'd never insist. But I will be your shadow any time you're here."

"I can live with that." I smile. "And for the record, if you insisted, I'd probably cave. But thank you for not making me."

"I should probably get you to Grace so she can check out the cuts you got," he says with malice in his tone. "I can't believe he cut you."

"Cuts heal."

"But they leave scars."

"Do you care about scars?"

"No, not the physical ones. But the mental ones... Yeah, I care about those. I don't want you to hurt in any way."

"I'll be okay."

"Kennedy?"

"Hmm?"

"I love you," he breathes. "I love you so damn much. I have from the second I saw you. My soul knew, my heart knew... I fucking love you, and I'll be gutted when you decide to walk away."

"Who says I'm walking away?"

"You don't want a relationship."

"Dip, we've been in a relationship from the start. No matter how I try to define it, I come back to that. I didn't think I'd want that, but it turns out, I was wrong. I want you, all of you."

"Fucking hell, woman."

"I love you too."

"Say it again," he demands.

"Ya know, Jenny said something to me a while ago that resonated in the deepest parts of me."

"Say it again," he repeats.

I grin. "She said, 'What if you find exactly what you never knew you wanted'."

"Kennedy," he growls. "Say. It. Again."

I lean into him.

"I love you, Dip. I found you, and I never even knew you were exactly what I wanted."

EPILOGUE

DIP

Two years later…

"Are you nervous?"

I look at Snow's reflection in the mirror next to mine and shake my head.

"Nope. I've been waiting for this day way too fucking long."

"She's been your ol' lady for two years, brother," he says with a chuckle. "A wedding doesn't change anything but making it legal."

After we dealt with *that fuck's* body, Jenny agreed to shut Barlow's down until we could secure another location. It didn't take long, which is good because she denied Little Man sex until the location was found. Poor guy went nuts for a whole week and a half.

It would've only been a week, but Kennedy begged me to take her back to Rhode Island so she could settle her husband's estate. She wanted to surprise Jenny with something, but she needed the money first.

Fortunately, Michael's attorney had been trying to track her down. Turns out, Michael had requested everything be sold upon his death, and all money transferred into an account in Kennedy's name. All Kennedy had to do was sign, and the money was hers.

While we were there, I asked her if she wanted to see her parents, and she said no. They've since both passed away, in a car accident, but she didn't seem all that bothered by it. As she put it, her past life was finally gone, history.

All we can do is move forward, Dip. Together. I refuse to feel sad about people who never felt sad for me.

We got back to Denver just in the knick of time, too, because Jenny was at the bank, ready to sign on the dotted line for the mortgage when Kennedy barreled in and tore up the contract.

"What the hell, Kennedy," Jenny cries. "I need to get my business back up and running."

"I know." Kennedy pulls an envelope out of her purse and hands it to her friend. "I'd like to be your partner."

"You... What?" Jenny slides her eyes to me. "Is she for real?"

"Open the envelope and find out," I tell her.

Jenny does and pulls out a cashier's check, made out to her, in the amount of three hundred grand.

"Kennedy, that's a lot of money."

"Jenny, you were my first real friend. You gave me a job, a place to live, and you wanted nothing in return. I want to do this."

"Partners, huh?"

"If you're okay with that."

Jenny was very okay with that. Now Barlow's is the

hottest bar in Denver, and there's rarely a night they aren't packed to capacity.

The door to the bathroom opens, and Duck walks in. "We're all ready out here."

"Finally," I mumble.

Little Man, who was patched in a few weeks after Kennedy's attack, pushes past Duck with a frantic look on his face.

"What's wrong?" I ask.

"Jenny's getting antsy. The baby's crying, her milk is dropping, and she not so nicely demanded I come in here and find out what's taking so fucking long."

I throw my head back and laugh. Leave it to an ol' lady to turn a brother into a frenzied mess.

"Little Man, go tell your wife to calm down," Snow orders, but then he frowns. "Never mind. I need you breathing. Remind her that the rest of the kids are with Carnie during the ceremony, and he's very capable of feeding Ramsy his bottle. Then get your ass to the altar. You're the goddamn best man." Snow turns to me. "And you, let's go get you hitched, brother."

It takes another forty minutes before the ceremony starts. Not only did Jenny nix the idea of Carnie feeding Ramsy, but Kennedy insisted she sit with Jenny while she nursed.

Women.

Snow officiates, having gotten ordained online. Kennedy wanted nothing to do with a church wedding, and she took it upon herself to ask Snow to stand in for a pastor. Of course, Snow agreed. Bikers might be badasses, but we're nothing if not accommodating to the women in our family.

"Do you, Kennedy, take Carson to be your old man?"

Kennedy beams. "I do."

"Do you, Carson, take Kennedy to be your ol' lady?"

"Fuck yes, I do."

"Yeah he does," Little Man adds from beside me, and we all laugh.

"Then by the power vested in me by the internet, I now pronounce you man and wife. Dip, you ma—"

I grab Kennedy's face and haul her lips to mine. She digs her nails into my chest, clinging to me as I kiss her passionately. Snow was wrong about one thing: a wedding didn't just make things legal.

Kissing Kennedy, *my wife*, is different... It's sweeter. Kissing my ol' lady is intoxicating, and I'll do it happily for the rest of my life, but sometimes, I need to remind her that she's my queen, not just my partner.

"I hate to break this up," Brady says as he strolls forward from his seat. "But I just got an alert from the security system mainframe."

I pull away from Kennedy, and she whimpers. "I'm not going," I assure her.

"You better not," she quips. "It's our wedding day."

"I know." I turn to Toga and Magic, who are sitting in the front row of chairs we set up in the park. "Can you two handle this?" I ask.

I've been fully in charge of the security system in the city, and Snow defers to me when it comes to anything regarding that. He's been delegating a lot more lately. He's the best president, but he's also a husband and father, and as important as the club is, family should take priority whenever it can.

"We're on it," they say in unison.

Since we rolled out the system across the city, crime has

gone down significantly. Ninety percent of the businesses downtown have let us take over their security, and we even made a deal with the police force where they'd look the other way if we had to dish out our brand of vigilante justice.

Of course, the very large donation we made to the department didn't hurt. Not to mention the fact that letting us do our thing allows them to have a better chance of going home to their families at night.

Knowing that Toga and Magic will handle whatever the alert was for, I return my attention to Kennedy.

"Are you hungry?" I ask her.

"Starving," she groans. "Do you have any idea how little I've eaten today to make sure this dress fit?"

Our guests start to head to the pavilion, where we'll have a buffet style meal and do all that wedding cake bull-shit. Then we'll head back to the clubhouse for the real party to begin.

I lean forward and nip at her ear. "You look stunning."

"Thank you."

"Let's go eat."

We walk hand in hand to join everyone. Kids are running around playing, adults are stuffing their faces, and I soak it all in. I always knew I wanted a family, I just never dreamed it would include so many people.

Life doesn't get much better than this.

"Dip?"

"Yeah?"

"I love you."

"I love you too."

"Kennedy!" Jenny calls from her seat at a picnic table. "Hurry up so we can cut the cake."

"We're coming," she shouts back.

"Is she pregnant again?" I ask. "Because she craved cake like crazy when she was."

"I don't think so," Kennedy says. "But God help Little Man if she is."

We take a few more steps, but then Kennedy digs in her heels and forces me to stop.

"Dip?"

"Yeah?" I ask, turning back to look at her.

Kennedy averts her eyes, which she hasn't done in so damn long.

"Kennedy," I growl.

When she looks at me, her irises sparkle with unshed tears, but she's smiling.

"Dip, I think I'm craving cake."

IF YOU LOVED SATAN'S LEGACY MC, CHECK OUT SOULLESS KINGS MC:

Fender: Book #1

Fender...

One night. That's all it takes for a person's life to forever be changed. One chaotic, unexpected, inevitable night and hundreds of bullets, two of them hitting my parents. I was born to be a Soulless King, born with sworn enemies and a loyal streak. Like a phoenix, I rise from the ash and vow to bring hell upon those responsible.

The problem with my vow is I'm not sure who is to blame. They tell me it's the temptress with emerald eyes, the one who used to share my bed. How can I be sure since she left without giving me the chance to find out the truth?

Now that she's back, she won't get away before I ask my questions. But what if I don't like the answers?

Charlie...

As the princess of the Black Savages, I was raised to believe one thing: my club is my family, no matter what. But when they are responsible for shattering the life I created, I do the only thing I can. I run.

The thing about running is I can't do it forever. Life, past transgressions, tragedy... they hunt me down and drag me back, shoving me into the deep end of fate. And fate is a fickle bitch.

What if my fate is with *him*, the president of the Black Savages' sworn enemy?

FENDER: PROLOGUE

They say your life flashes before your eyes at the moment just before death. They fucking lied.

Fender

Slick.

Wet.

Hot.

Perfect.

That's the only way to describe the pussy I'm buried in. Charlie moans and the sound seems to echo around us in flawless rhythm with the headboard banging against the wall.

"That's it, baby," I growl as I reach between our bodies and rub circles over her clit with my thumb.

Charlie's eyes resemble an emerald in its purest form, and I'm lost, drowning in a sea of green. They widen and her pupils dilate the second her orgasm begins. Tingles race down my spine, and my body tenses as I join her.

We explode together, and the sounds we've created die

down. My heart is pounding, and her breathing is labored. I roll off of her, carrying her with me and tucking her into my side.

"Holy shit, Fender."

"What?" I ask, a grin tugging at my lips. She always says the same thing after we fuck. Always.

"It gets better every—"

"Fender, get the fuck out here!"

The pounding on my door and the urgency in Piston's voice has me springing from the bed and grabbing my gun from the nightstand. That's when it registers. Gunshots, yelling, glass shattering.

"Fender! Now!" Piston's fist is an inch away from my face when I throw open the door. "Black Savages stormed the club. Get dressed and c'mon!"

I glance over my shoulder and see Charlie shoving her legs into her jeans. Her ass is encased in the black lace I pulled off her body with my teeth not a half hour ago. I hate to see her cover her flesh, but I can't think about that right now.

"Get in the fuckin' closet and don't come out. Not for anything." I grip her bicep and drag her to the door in the corner of the room, throw it open and shove her in.

"Maybe I can talk to them. Maybe I—"

"No. They're past talking and so am I." I crush her lips in a bruising kiss before shutting the door in her face.

I dress as quickly as I can and mentally prepare for what I'm about to face. Certainly nothing good. I make my way down the hall, my gun cocked and ready to blow away any Savage that gets in my path.

I just pray it's not Dyno. It would be great to take out the president of the Black Savages, but I can't do that to Charlie. I can't kill her dad.

I round the corner into the main room of the clubhouse and am shocked at the carnage. The floor is littered with broken liquor bottles and booze. There's also blood and bodies, and it's hard to tell what club the deceased belong to.

"Fender!"

I whirl toward the voice and see my father, his shirt soaked in blood, kneeling on the floor. My mother is cocooned in his arms, her body limp. Everything else melts away. The shouting, the gunfire, the mayhem. Cold calm washes over me as I walk toward my parents, ignoring the bullets whizzing past my head. Maybe I'd get lucky, and one would take me out so I wouldn't have to face what I know is coming.

Time speeds up the closer I get. I drop to my knees. "Where are you hit?"

My father's stare is blank, empty. When he doesn't respond, I run my hands over his chest to determine if the blood is his or all from the hole I can now see in my mother's head. I don't allow myself to feel the loss. I can't afford to fall apart right now. My fingers hit a soft spot, a hole, on the left side of my father's chest. I rip the sleeves from his shirt and stuff the fabric in the hole to slow the bleeding. He hisses in pain, but that's his only reaction.

"Stay here," I shout at him, praying he hears what I'm saying. "I'll be back."

I lunge to my feet and storm into the middle of the room. I take a deep breath and find my first target. I point the gun and squeeze the trigger, not stopping until I've systematically taken out every Black Savage still standing, emptying the clip in the process.

"What the fuck was that?" Piston asks, walking through the bodies, kicking a few as he goes.

"Who'd we lose?" I survey the scene, trying to answer my own question.

"Stunner, Carbon, Phantom," Piston rubs his head, leaving a streak of blood. He's looking around, same as me. His head stops moving, and his gaze lands on something behind me. "Aw, fuck."

I slowly turn around, needing to see what he sees, and instantly regret it. My father is slumped over, both my parents dead. It's fitting, I suppose. They lived for the club and died for it. It's what they would've wanted, to go out together in a blaze of glory.

Bang!

I pivot around at the gunshot, shocked to hear it because I thought the chaos was over. Charlie's standing there, her eyes wide, her arms straight, the gun in her hand. I follow her gaze to the man she just killed. Sharp, the Black Savages' Sergeant at Arms, is lying on the floor with a bullet hole between his eyes.

"He was gonna kill you," she mumbles.

"You need to leave," Piston demands. "You don't belong here."

My eyes dart back and forth between the woman I love and my best friend. He's absolutely right. She shouldn't be here. Especially now. But I don't have it in me to make her leave.

"Did you do this?" Joker shouts from behind Piston, directing the question at Charlie. "Precious Black Savages' princess coordinates Soulless Kings' massacre. Isn't spreading your legs enough to secure your place?"

Charlie's arms drop to her sides, and the gun clanks to the floor. She's staring at me, silently begging me to defend her, protect her from the lies my brother's spewing. Problem is, I can't. What if he's right?

"Get the fuck out!" Joker shouts, pointing toward the exit.

Charlie's eyes well with tears as she turns and runs out the front door. In my twenty-three years on this Earth, I've stared down the barrel of a gun more times than I can count, and it doesn't hold a candle to what I'm experiencing right now.

I was born to be a Soulless King, raised to be a ruthless, loyal motherfucker. None of that prepared me for this moment. Nothing could make losing so much any easier to swallow.

They say your life flashes before your eyes at the moment just before death. They fucking lied.

Your life flashes before your eyes at the moment you lose everything you live for.

ABOUT THE AUTHOR

Andi Rhodes is an author whose passion is creating romance from chaos in all her books! She writes MC (motorcycle club) romance with a generous helping of suspense and doesn't shy away from the more difficult topics. Her books can be triggering for some so consider yourself warned. Andi also ensures each book ends with the couple getting their HEA! Most importantly, Andi is living her real life HEA with her husband and their boxers.

ALSO BY ANDI RHODES

Broken Rebel Brotherhood

Broken Souls

Broken Innocence

Broken Boundaries

Broken Rebel Brotherhood: Complete Series Box set

Broken Rebel Brotherhood: Next Generation

Broken Hearts

Broken Wings

Broken Mind

Bastards and Badges

Stark Revenge

Slade's Fall

Jett's Guard

Soulless Kings MC

Fender

Joker

Piston

Greaser

Riker

Trainwreck

Squirrel

Gibson

Flash

Royal

Satan's Legacy MC

Snow's Angel

Toga's Demons

Magic's Torment

Duck's Salvation

Dip's Flame

Devil's Handmaidens MC

Harlow's Gamble

Peppermint's Twist

Mama's Rules

Valhalla Rising MC

Viking

Mayhem Makers

Forever Savage

Saints Purgatory MC

Unholy Soul

Printed in Great Britain
by Amazon